Pre-Fall Marriage

God's Original Will

A Journey by Email
to a
Mutually Satisfying
Marriage

Rick and Georgeann Mills

PreFallMarriage.com
or
https://www.facebook.com/PreFallMarriage

Version 1.00

Cover artwork: Marriages Through the Fire

ISBN 978-0-9862236-0-0

RF Publishing
Ames, IA 50014

ALSO BY RICK AND GEORGEANN MILLS

Pre-Fall Marriage God's Original Will: A Workbook of
Main Points and Probing Questions

https://Pre-FallMarriage.com

ALSO BY RICK MILLS

The Yoke of Jesus: If His Yoke is Easy,
Why Can Life Be So Difficult

https://TheYokeOfJesus.com

Table of Contents

PREFACE

This novel is about Jack and Caroline's journey with Rick and Georgeann Mills to a Pre-Fall mutually satisfying marriage. While its purpose is primarily to help married and engaged couples with their personal and marriage-related struggles, individuals in various types and stages of relationships will also find this material beneficial.

People who are divorced can use this material to not only understand relationships from their past, but also to build a mutually satisfying marriage in the future. People who are single can use this material to understand the mental and emotional dynamics of their current and past relationships, as well as the relationships of others such as parents, family, and friends. And finally, anyone who is committed to helping couples heal and grow through marriage will find this novel to be a useful resource.

Fictional experiences are described in this novel that for some will be unpleasant to read, and for others, painful to remember. Our purpose is not to open mental and emotional wounds unnecessarily, but rather, it is to shed light on areas that can cause pain and difficulty in marriage. The pain and difficulty that many couples go through is not surprising based on the marriages they have seen, and the role models who taught them what to think and how to act in a marriage. We are hopeful the light that is offered in this novel brings clarity.

Even though you can benefit from reading this novel on your own, we encourage you to read it with your spouse, a friend, or a study group, so together, you can pray and work through the thoughts and feelings that arise. It is often in the eyes of someone you trust that the truth of your past experiences is reflected more accurately than what you can perceive on your own. That said, anything from someone else that you receive into your thinking must be in alignment with Scripture, and also be consistent with your discernment from the Holy Spirit.

This novel provides educational insight and is not offered as a therapeutic process or any form of therapy. If reading it triggers strong and potentially overwhelming emotions from your current or past circumstances, please take a break from reading, put yourself first, and establish a therapeutic relationship with a qualified mental health professional.

If you ever feel like you may physically harm yourself or someone else, call a trusted family member, friend, Christian brother or sister, pastor, counselor, or psychiatrist. In an emergency, either call your local emergency service (usually 9-1-1 in the United States), or a law enforcement agency. You may also go to the nearest emergency room on your own, or have someone take you. You are precious in God's eyes and worthy of the care you need.

All characters in this novel are fictional except for Rick and Georgeann. Any other names, characters, businesses, places, events, locales, and incidents are either the products of Rick or Georgeann's imagination, or used in a fictitious manner. Specific references to people or events are used by permission.

As part of our desire to continue with you on your journey to a Pre-Fall mutually satisfying marriage, we have a companion website, **https://Pre-FallMarriage.com,** and a page on Facebook, **https://www.facebook.com/PreFallMarriage**. At these two sites we will periodically offer additional thoughts on marriage based on our personal growth, and comments from you and others. If you have insights or helpful suggestions that you would like to share, we would love to hear from you.

Blessings by the power of the Holy Spirit on your journey to build a mutually satisfying marriage,

Rick and Georgeann

DEDICATION

This novel is dedicated to you as you live out your journey of healing and growth through a mutually satisfying marriage. Your courage and the choices you make will change your destiny and the destiny of your family and others for generations. You matter and your healing and growth matters to God as He conforms you into your unique image of Jesus. The mutually satisfying marriage that you build with your spouse matters to a watching world who needs hope, direction, and peace.

May God bless you as you grow in wisdom, gentleness, and perseverance on your journey.

OVERVIEW

In this novel, Jack and Caroline are missionaries serving in a very remote location with intermittent connectivity to the internet. They love each other, but argue constantly. They will not be coming back to the States until they complete their current tour, and have asked Rick and Georgeann for help. Since the four of them cannot meet face to face, and the use of video conferencing is impossible, Rick and Georgeann have agreed to attempt the very unusual task of helping them by email. The result is an exchange of emails about God's purpose for healing and growth through their marriage, and how Jack's and Caroline's wounds and defenses contribute to their arguments. Jack and Caroline learn strategies and tools for building a mutually satisfying marriage. They also receive a Conflict Checklist for identifying factors that are contributing to their arguments.

Pre-Fall Marriage

God made his original will for Adam and Eve's relationship clear when He said,

> ..."Let us make mankind in our image, in our likeness, so that they may rule over the fish in the sea and the birds in the sky, over the livestock and all the wild animals, and over all the creatures that move along the ground." [27] So God created mankind in his own image, in the image of God he created them; male and female he created them. (Genesis 1:26-27)

The "mankind" to which God referred was Adam and Eve, and together they were given rule "over the fish in the sea and the birds in the sky, over the livestock and all the wild animals, and over all the creatures that move along the ground." Adam's rule over Eve came only after the Fall when Satan injected his will into the Garden, causing God to speak to them in Genesis 3:16. "'To the woman he said, "I will make your pains in childbearing very severe; with painful labor you will give birth to children. Your desire will be for your husband, and he will rule over you."'

The beauty, love, and power that was built into Adam and Eve as the image of the "us" who were present with God at creation became distorted into a struggle for power in the presence of pain. What happened to God's original will for marriage?

In the Sermon on the Mount, Jesus taught what has become known as the Lord's Prayer.

> "This, then, is how you should pray:
> "'Our Father in heaven, hallowed be your name,
> [10] your kingdom come, your will be done,
>   on earth as it is in heaven.
> [11] Give us today our daily bread.
> [12] And forgive us our debts,
>   as we also have forgiven our debtors.
> [13] And lead us not into temptation,
>   but deliver us from the evil one.' (Matthew 6:9-13)

When Jesus said in verse 10, "your kingdom come, your will be done on earth as it is in heaven," we think He meant this literally. But, this raises the question, "What is God's heavenly will for an earthly marriage?"

We believe that God's heavenly will for an earthly marriage is to build it on a Pre-Fall foundation where spouses are once again coequal in their created image of God. This stands in direct contrast to those who advocate building a marriage on the fallen rubble of first century Roman culture where a wife was the property of her husband.

A problem arises, however, in that there isn't a lot recorded in Scripture about the rules and behaviors that Adam and Eve were to live by in their Pre-Fall marriage. And, why would there be?

They knew all they needed to know, and what they knew was all good. They were without sin because of their lack of knowledge about good and evil. They had no selfish desires, unmet needs, fears, wounds, defenses, or assumptions. Today, such is not the case for Christians and their marriages.

Even though people become a new creation when they accept Jesus as their Savior, God retains their old brain. This brain has a mind that includes finely tuned time-tested rules, behaviors, and instincts for survival. These instincts are near-instantaneous in their reaction time, and are driven by desires, needs, fears, past and present wounds, defenses, and assumptions. A transformation of this mind and these instincts is needed.

God wants your desires purified, needs met, fears confronted, wounds healed, defenses removed, and assumptions challenged. He wants your instincts reexamined, your rules rewritten, and your behaviors redirected so you can walk in wisdom, love, self-discipline, and power. (2 Timothy 1:7). In fact, God's will is the same for everyone in that He wants to conform each of us into our own unique image of Jesus. (Romans 8:29)

One of the tools God uses to bring about this conformation is a marriage relationship. To that end, we believe a primary purpose of marriage is healing and growth, and that one spouse's desires and needs can be signals for areas in which God wants the other to grow. It is by this growth that those desires and needs can be met. This begins with both spouses offering themselves to God as a living sacrifice.

> Therefore, I urge you, brothers and sisters, in view of God's mercy, to offer your bodies as a living sacrifice, holy and pleasing to God—this is your true and proper worship. 2 Do not conform to the pattern of this world, but be transformed by the renewing of your mind. Then you will be able to test and approve what God's will is—his good, pleasing and perfect will. (Romans 12:1-2)

Many people *go to* God's altar to pray for what is on their mind, and when finished, leave and work hard at bringing about what they desire. In essence, they ask God to bless their efforts the way rain blesses a farmer. This is not what Romans 12:1-2 is urging.

God wants you to *climb up onto* His altar and offer yourself as a *living* sacrifice. This is the kind of worship that pleases Him. It allows Him to address the ways you have been conformed to this world, and it allows Him to transform you by renewing your mind. As your mind is renewed, you will become more and more confident in knowing what He wants you to do.

God does not want you *working for Him*, rather, He wants to *work through you*. This does not take away your freedom and responsibility, rather, it frees you to respond to God as your loving Father and not as a harsh taskmaster. When God works through you as you rest in Him, you arise with love, strength, and power.

So where is the specific guidance found in the Bible for spouses who want to build a Pre-Fall marriage? It is the same guidance that Scripture offers on how we as Christians should interact with one another and those around us.

We believe God wants husbands to treat their wives at least as well and even better than they treat anyone else, and He wants wives to do the same with their husbands. Therefore, Scriptures such as Luke 6:27 that say you should love your enemies could be appended with, "… and love your spouse with the same love and even more than what I am commanding you to have for your enemies." Scriptures such as Ephesians 4:15 that say you should speak the truth in love could be appended with, "… and speak the truth to your spouse with the same love and even more than you should have for a fellow believer." This means that specific guidance for a Pre-Fall marriage is found throughout Scripture.

An invitation

We welcome you to join us, Jack, and Caroline, as they embark on their journey by email to a mutually satisfying Pre-Fall marriage. If you do, there are at least six requirements for success: desire, opportunity, time, energy, courage, and insight.

Both you and your spouse must grow in your *desire* for a

mutually satisfying marriage and be willing to offer each other the *opportunity* for connection. If one or both of you are closed off mentally and/or emotionally to the other, your journey is in peril. Both of you must also set aside *time* for this journey, and allow the Holy Spirit to work in and through you as He provides the *energy*.

In addition, both of you need to grow in your *courage* to examine your past relationships and the impact that those relationships have had on you and your current relationships. Each of you must also grow in your *courage* to examine your mental and emotional struggles as individuals and as a couple.

And finally, you will need *insight* into your automatic survival instincts that protect your mental and emotional wounds. We can provide some insight with this novel, and you must either bring or be willing to grow in the other requirements.

Companion workbook of main points and probing questions

We have also written a companion workbook titled, Pre-Fall Marriage God's Original Will – A Workbook of Main Points and Probing Questions. The main points and probing questions are organized according to the emails in this novel. The questions are also divided into Me Questions to be answered individually, and We Questions to be answered as a couple. There is also a Your Thoughts section after each set of questions.

If you and your spouse use the workbook, success will not be achieved merely by reading through the main points and questions. It is by reading, thinking, praying, working through the questions, discussing, and putting your insights into practice that the two of you will experience the often painful process of healing and growth, along with the joyful process of building and experiencing your own mutually satisfying marriage.

Try not to lose sight of the fact that even though God's path for your journey will be painful, the outcome of healing and growth and of being conformed to your unique image of Jesus is worth it.

In Him,

Rick and Georgeann

Subject: Hello

Dear Rick and Georgeann,

Jack is visiting villages for the next couple of days and our kids are napping so I thought this would be a good time to email you for the both of us. Words cannot express our gratitude for your willingness to help us with our marriage.

Even though I have never met the two of you, I feel like I know you through Beth's emails. For about a year she's been telling me how much you have helped her and Bob with their marriage. What caused us to finally ask her to see if we could contact you was what we saw at a family gathering during our recent furlough.

Beth and Bob actually looked at each other when they talked. He treated her in a way that showed she really mattered to him. And, Beth showed affection in return by touching him on his arm when he would walk by. It was like having my big sister back. We even saw them get into a disagreement that didn't end in an argument. That is totally new. If you can do for us what you have done for them, it would be nothing short of a miracle.

I'm not sure how much you and Georgeann know about us, so I'll fill you in on some of our background. We have been married for eleven years and have two children. Our son Billy is nine and our daughter Erica is seven. This is our second tour, and we will not be returning for another fifteen months.

Jack and I come from two very different families. Jack's family is reserved with almost a total lack of affection. I have never even seen his mother and father touch each other. My family on the other hand, as you know from Beth, is very affectionate. We hug every time we leave, come home, or even when we go to bed. And if anyone leaves or comes home from a trip, it's time for doubles or triples!

Jack and I wanted to be missionaries beginning in high school, which is part of what attracted us to each other. Jack always talked about making a difference in the world, and my heart is geared towards preventing pain and easing suffering. He would plan and carryout community outreach activities, and I would fill in by doing what was needed when it was needed. It seemed like we were a perfect fit, but now it feels like all we do is argue. He is constantly worrying, and I keep telling him we need to trust God.

Jack agrees we are struggling in our marriage, and I think what upsets him the most is that he can't fix it. He fixes everything. He just fixed our four-wheeler, our roof, and the outside well. He helps build housing for the villagers, and even set up a water purification system that was delivered by another ministry to a village ten miles North of ours. He is amazing. With everything he has to do and the unbelievable amount of pressure he is under, I hate myself for telling him I am unhappy. I feel so guilty.

Last night we had another devastating argument that started in our typical hushed voices to prevent our children and neighbors from hearing. Unfortunately, it didn't stay that way and they seldom do.

I was frustrated and unhappy because I hadn't seen much of him for nearly three weeks. The children were missing him and I was too. He went into his rational explanation of all he had to do. I asked, "But what about me and the kids?" In his typical defensive, distant, and unemotional tone he countered with his classic style of interrogation. "Do you want me to give up our ministry? Who else is going to do all of this? You? Do you want to preach this Sunday?" I got angry and emotional, which he always dismisses as weakness.

His anger kept building as he pointed out that we both agreed to go on this tour, and that he was doing everything possible to serve God, raise support, keep a roof over our heads, and be a good father. He finally lost his composure and yelled, "What more do you want?!" I couldn't speak. He yelled even louder, "What more do you want?!!" Tears began rolling down my face and eventually all I could say was, "I want you." He took a couple of steps forward looking me directly in the eyes. Finally, he said slowly and deliberately, "You can't have me." He turned and walked out of the room. I just stood there. I have never felt so alone.

When I got up this morning he had already made coffee and was reading his Bible. I could tell he had been crying. We talked and he apologized for saying, in his words, "such a stupid thing." He said he loved me and wanted to do whatever it took to make me happy. I told him I knew he loved me and that I forgave him. We definitely want to move forward together with the help the two of you are offering.

With hope,

Caroline

P.S. We set up this joint email account so both of us will see what you write to either of us. We do not want secrets between us. If an email or a section of an email is written by one of us, we will start by identifying who it is.

Subject: Re: Hello; Couples, Spinning Plates, and Happiness

Caroline and Jack, this is Rick.

It is highly unusual for us to try to help without meeting with the two of you in person. We usually meet with couples twice a week for the first two weeks and then once a week after that. A typical session lasts two to three hours. We do this because it takes time to get to know one another, and for us to cover the background concepts that characterize our approach. It also lets us answer questions in real-time and adjust our explanations as needed. We will do our best to be as thorough as we can, but this approach will likely result in some very long emails. In our effort to anticipate and answer your questions, we will try not to be too tedious in our explanations. We wish we could do this by video conferencing, but based on what Beth told us about where you are serving, even intermittent access to email is a luxury.

Last week I was talking with a friend about the four of us trying to work together using only email. She is very familiar with our work and was concerned that keeping track of various topics throughout a series of emails would be difficult. Her suggestion was to use headers for each topic. I respect her opinions and will give it a try. Feel free to do the same with your replies as long as it doesn't impose too much of a burden. If it gets too distracting we can stop. After all, it's not like we're writing a book.

We are far from being experts in marriage. Our most meaningful credential is that for over forty-three years we have had many successes in our marriage and paid particular attention to our mistakes. We have also paid attention to the successes and mistakes of other couples. As a result, what we offer is what has worked for us and others who are on the same journey of building a mutually satisfying marriage.

You can learn from us, but please do not try to imitate our relationship. God has his own design for the two of you. That said, much of what we have learned will be helpful. By the way, if you find anything we write to be too overwhelming, or at some point you decide you would rather not continue, just let us know.

Couples do the work

Georgeann and I listen very carefully to the words people choose because words often carry deep and subtle meanings. Please forgive us if we over-interpret what you write.

We noticed in your email that you used the phrase "do for us what you have done for them," and the word "miracle" when you wrote, "If you can do for us what you have done for them, it would be nothing short of a miracle." Fortunately for us, we really don't do all that much work relative to what our couples do.

Ultimately, all we really do is provide a different perspective and awareness, surface God's wisdom, provide our own honest stories of success and failure, and facilitate the moving of the Holy Spirit. What makes the real difference is the courage, humility, and hard work that couples bring, and their willingness to submit to God's insight and wisdom in the power of the Holy Spirit. All of this is what enables them to face longstanding:

- desires
- needs
- fears
- wounds
- defenses
- assumptions

The first night Bob and Beth came over, we could tell they were nervous and filled with apprehension. We told them it took a tremendous amount of courage to come through our door the first time, and it would take even more the second. Obviously, they came back, and have given us permission to share with you anything about them that we think may be helpful.

A couple or not a couple

One of the first things we try to figure out when two people come to us is if they are truly a "couple." Being a couple means they are not in an abusive relationship where the power struggle is for one spouse to *deform* the other into what he or she wants without regard for that person's desires and needs. This type of mentally, emotionally, spiritually, and/or physically abusive relationship is not a "couple." It is one or both people trying to manipulate the other. Their goal is to have all of their:

- desires met

- needs satisfied

- fears silenced

- wounds avoided

- defenses unchallenged

- assumptions validated

These abusers assume that their spouse was placed on this earth to serve them. In this circumstance, an abuser must first receive effective individual counseling before entering into couples counseling. Since we refuse to collude with an abuser's goal of subjugating his or her spouse, he or she usually does not stay around us very long.

A couple, however, is willing to consider how each person may contribute to a conflict without necessarily being wrong. A couple is willing to entertain the idea that each other's perspective may have merit worth understanding. They know their relationship is painful, and each is open to the idea that some sort of change is necessary. They both are willing to listen and be heard in the context of mental, emotional, spiritual, and physical safety. Of course, there are no perfect relationships, and they vary from time to time along this continuum of safety. Our goal for all couples is that they know each other deeply and that their relationship becomes an increasingly safer refuge for healing and growth.

Bob and Beth are definitely a couple because they continually work hard to understand each other. They learned that the majority of their arguments stemmed directly from their unmet desires, unacknowledged needs, unresolved fears, past wounds, clashing defenses, and unyielding assumptions. And, these were often amplified by their daily pressures. We know this can sound complicated, and it is! So, where is God and His will in all of this?

God's will for each of us and a purpose for marriage

God wants our desires purified, needs met, fears confronted, wounds healed, defenses removed, and assumptions examined. He wants all of us to walk in wisdom according to 2 Timothy 1:7, " For the Spirit God gave us does not make us timid, but gives us power, love and self-discipline." In addition, God's will is the same for all of us as recorded in Romans 8:29, "For those God foreknew he also predestined to be conformed to the image of his Son, that he might be the firstborn among many brothers and sisters." This means that God is continuously conforming the two of you, Beth, Bob, Georgeann and me into our own unique image of Jesus.

One of the tools God uses to bring about this conformation is a marriage relationship. To that end, we believe a primary purpose of marriage is for healing and growth, and that one spouse's desires and needs can be signals for areas in which God wants the other to grow. It is by this growth that those desires and needs can be met. That's why, Caroline, it concerned me when you wrote, "He is under an unbelievable amount of pressure and I hate myself for telling him I am unhappy. I feel so guilty."

A spouse's desire is often a need for the relationship

Rather than feel guilty for your unhappiness, we encourage you to embrace it with gentleness and purpose. Ask God to give you insight into your desires and needs. If you do not tell Jack about a felt desire or need, rather than *sacrificing for* your relationship by avoiding confrontation, you could actually be *doing harm* to your relationship by setting the stage for even more conflict in the future. Obviously, a manipulative spouse can abuse this principle of expressing desires and needs, but for couples it rarely is a problem.

Unfortunately, people who do not understand that a primary purpose of marriage is healing and growth, often think its purpose is to satisfy all of their desires, many of which are holdovers from childhood. A hidden desire often is, "Ah, finally someone to love me like my mother and father should have." Or, "All of my childhood insecurities will go away because I have found the perfect spouse to satisfy my desires." When after several years of marriage these desires are not fulfilled and the insecurities remain, it is easy for them to feel betrayed and ripped off by their spouse who was expected to be the perfect match. This is when one or both spouses can either look for a *better deal* with someone else, or muster the courage through the power of the Holy Spirit to face their real desires, needs, fears, wounds, defenses, and assumptions.

Courageously reexamine everything

Bob and Beth responded to their pain by courageously reexamining everything about themselves and their relationship in the light of God's truth. It wasn't that all of their desires were selfish, all of their needs were permanent, all of their fears were unjustified, all of their wounds were imagined, all of their defenses were unnecessary, or all of their assumptions were unreasonable. The problem was that these often got in the way of what they wanted more, which was a satisfying marriage. Challenging all of these is painful, messy, frustrating, rewarding, and according to them…worth it.

We often had to remind Bob and Beth that it had taken a lifetime to get where they were, and it would take time, commitment, and hard work for their relationship to recover and grow into what they wanted. Some of their previous experiences were helpful, while others, not so much.

Insight, tools, and being a living sacrifice

Every couple has a choice to either deal with their pain, or pass it on to their children and others. What saddens us deeply is that many couples do not have the necessary insight and tools to work through their painful past and its current impact on their marriage. They are clueless about how to build a healthy marriage. They are like people who try to build a house without plans, while using their forehead as a hammer. Eventually the pain becomes too great to continue.

Our life's work is to provide insight and tools that couples can use in the power of the Holy Spirit to build their marriage in a way that God intended. This begins with both people offering themselves to God as a living sacrifice.

> Therefore, I urge you, brothers and sisters, in view of God's mercy, to offer your bodies as a living sacrifice, holy and pleasing to God — this is your true and proper worship. ² Do not conform to the pattern of this world, but be transformed by the renewing of your mind. Then you will be able to test and approve what God's will is — his good, pleasing and perfect will. (Romans 12:1-2)

Many people *go to* God's altar to pray for what is on their mind, and when finished, leave and work hard to bring about what they desire. In essence, they ask God to bless their efforts in the way rain blesses a farmer. This is not what Romans 12:1-2 is urging.

God wants us to *climb up onto* His altar and offer ourselves as a *living* sacrifice. This is the kind of worship that pleases Him. It allows Him to address the ways we have been conformed to this world, and allows Him to transform us by the renewing of our mind. As our mind is renewed, we will become more and more confident in what He wants us to do.

God does not want us *working for Him*, rather, He wants to *work through us*. This does not take away our freedom and responsibility, rather, it frees us to respond to God as our loving Father and not as a harsh taskmaster. When we rest in Him, we arise with love, strength, and power.

Jack,

Spinning plates

It sounds like you have a lot of responsibilities and are under a great deal of pressure. I remember those days well and they were not fun. I once described them to a friend that it was like having spinning plates on sticks that I would have to run from one to another to keep them spinning so they wouldn't fall. Every time I looked up, either several plates were beginning to wobble, or two or three new plates had mysteriously been added.

My biggest mistake was viewing my wife, children, and even God as just more plates that needed spinning. I felt like they always needed something and would not keep spinning long enough for me to catch my breath. I kept getting more and more tired, frustrated, and impatient. Vince Lombardi once said, "Fatigue makes cowards of us all." I don't know about it making me a "coward," but it did make me feel angry, inadequate, and at times, mean. I suspect that is what motivated your comment about Caroline not being allowed to have you. Try not to be too hard on yourself brother, from time to time everyone says "stupid" things.

Making someone happy

When Caroline wrote, "He said he loved me and wanted to do whatever it took to make me happy," it raised a concern. No one can make another person happy, though our actions can definitely make someone unhappy with us. Caroline's happiness is something for which only she can be responsible. That is between her and God. You can only act in a godly loving way towards her, and it is her choice to respond appropriately.

We obviously do not know you well enough yet, so I'm not sure if what I'm about to write applies to you. I'm just working from Caroline's perspective regarding the argument she shared.

Expressing emotions

Caroline referred to your "rational explanation" and your "defensive, distant, and unemotional tone," along with her response of, "I got angry and emotional, which he always dismisses as weakness." This sounds like the rule, *Whoever gets emotional first...loses,* along with the obvious rationale that you can't reason with someone who is emotional. The problem is that emotional does not necessarily mean irrational and wrong. It can mean provoked and right.

In general, I dislike generalizations. Even so, what follows is consistent more often than not. Men often hide behind a seemingly righteous and unemotional shield of logic, while women are often looking for validation of their concerns and an emotional connection. Men often think they are not emotional if they do not express their emotions, yet women know those emotions exist and are often boiling under the surface.

When a husband values constraining his emotions, he often devalues his wife when she does not. He is likely to use this devaluation as a convenient excuse for dismissing her concerns. He might respond with statements such as, "If you want to talk about it rationally, we will. Otherwise, I won't." Or, "Even if you are right, which you aren't, the way you are expressing yourself is wrong." As I mentioned before, the problem often isn't with a wife being emotional, the problem is with her being provoked.

Another possible factor in your arguing and Caroline getting emotional is what has been referred to as the Still Face Experiment. It begins when a mother and her infant are face to face and smiling and cooing at each other. This sets up a connection of resonating feedback. One of them smiles and the other responds. According to the experiment, the mother looks away, changes the expression on her face to one of no emotion, and returns to looking directly into the baby's eyes. In response, the baby tries to be cute to reestablish the connection. When the mother remains expressionless, the baby gets frustrated, distressed, and angry; sometimes even striking out at the mother. When the mother responds once again with smiles and cooing, the baby is suspicious at first, then relieved, and settles back into a contented state once their resonating connection is reestablished.

I think adults can suffer from the same type of still-face provocation. When one spouse is perceived as cold and emotionally disconnected, the other can get anxious, irritated, and angry to the point of demanding a connection by becoming more and more emotional. This isn't particularly odd, it's just the way most people are wired for personal and social connection.

Remember, I don't know if any of this applies to you.

Caroline and Jack,

Long-term hope

Our long-term hope for the two of you is that once you are enjoying your marriage as God intended, you will minister to other couples. This is consistent with the desires the two of you had in high school of making a difference by ministering to others, relieving their pain, and preventing unnecessary suffering. After all, restoring a single marriage to what God intended, changes the destiny of that family and others for generations.

This email is longer than I thought it would be and it contains a lot of material for you to process. Please take your time and work through it at your own pace, as well as those that follow.

The real value in these emails is in how the two of you pray and talk through the insights contained in them, and how you put those insights into practice. Every day you will be offered a thousand other more urgent things to do. The problem is that each day that nothing changes, nothing changes.

We know the two of you are in pain, sometimes so much that you can barely move, but move you must. You must make the difficult choice to face your pain together. We can only offer insight and prayer; it's what the two of you do with this insight in the power of the Holy Spirit that will change your life and the lives of those you love. God will provide you with even more insights than what we give you, so please don't hesitate to share them with us so we can continue to improve our own marriage and the marriages of others.

Jack, what are your thoughts about the spinning plates that demand your continuous effort or they will fall? Do you see people as being like those plates? If you do, is God a plate?

Caroline, what are your thoughts about your needs?

In Him,

Rick

Subject: Arguing, Needs, Love, and Respect

Rick and Georgeann,

Jack isn't back yet, so it will be a couple of days before he responds.

Interesting that you picked up so quickly on our pattern for arguing. Jack is a passionate man, but he rarely expresses his emotions. Being open about feelings in his family was dangerous.

They debate anything and everything in their civil and condescending manner. And, no one ever admits they are wrong, even when it is obvious. They act like their unemotional words are less damaging than the more conventional yelling that other families do. In my opinion, yelling is far more honest.

I get so frustrated, angry, and even furious at times when Jack does this to me. Sometimes when I fight back I say things I deeply regret the next day. That's when I feel the most hopeless. Even if I am right, I am wrong. I have no idea how to change this.

It isn't surprising that you would ask me about my "needs" because this is an area Beth and I have been going around and around about lately. The Bible speaks very clearly about meeting my needs.

Ephesians 5:33 makes it clear women need love and men need respect when it reads, "However, each one of you also must love his wife as he loves himself, and the wife must respect her husband." I need Jack to love me and he needs my respect. As far as my daily needs are concerned, it is wrong for me to be preoccupied with them. I am supposed to look after the needs of others as Paul writes in Philippians,

> "Do nothing out of selfish ambition or vain conceit. Rather, in humility value others above yourselves, 4 not looking to your own interests but each of you to the interests of the others." (Philippians 2:3-4)

Even Jesus said,

"'It is more blessed to give than to receive.'" (Acts 20:35)

I also rely on Matthew 6:20 as my guide. "But store up for yourselves treasures in heaven, where moths and vermin do not destroy, and where thieves do not break in and steal." When I am seeking to have my needs fulfilled, I am not storing up treasures in heaven.

Sacrifice is a part of love and is essential in any healthy relationship. When you wrote in your previous email about me being conformed to the image of Jesus, what I saw was sacrifice. He sacrificed for us and we are supposed to do the same for others.

Besides, when I get focused on myself, it just makes me feel bad. To be absolutely honest, I hate it. I feel completely selfish. Ultimately, Jesus will take care of my needs. I choose to trust Him and not rely on people. Based on my conversations with Beth, I'm pretty sure you are going to tell me I am wrong.

By the way, in your first email you wrote that Bob and Beth said it was okay to share anything about them with us that you think would be helpful. In the same way, feel free to share anything with them about us. We are family and want to do whatever we can to help one another.

Sincerely,

Caroline

Subject: Your Observing Ego and Shame

Caroline, this is Rick.

Good to hear back from you so quickly. Let Jack know there is no rush for him to respond. I'm sure he will be tired when he gets back, and you and the kids will want to catch up on your time with him. I remember when our daughters were young and I would go to conferences. I tried to save some energy for the joyous onslaught when I returned.

This is a long email and I'm going to cover some topics that will seem odd this soon into our working together. Eventually they will make sense. Some of the points I will make are subtle and can sound a bit like heresy, so please read carefully.

Observing ego

Changing how we interact with others begins with the ability to accurately observe ourselves while we are in the process of interacting. Many authors refer to this capacity as an observing ego, which is our continuous awareness that observes our thoughts, emotions, and attitudes, as well as our strategies for getting what we want.

Some authors refer to the observing ego as one's conscience or "the parent within." Basically, our observing ego is a running narrative of our thoughts that comment on what we feel, think, say, and do. For example, my observing ego looks at this paragraph and wonders if I have made it clear enough, or does it sound too much like psycho-babble?

Those who refer to the observing ego as "the parent within" often make it sound like it is a separate person (a child's parent) that is imported into his or her mind that must either be accepted or rejected. Others refer to the observing ego as "tapes," which are today's equivalent of an MP3. These recordings, that play in their mind, sound like what their parents said to them when they were growing up, be it praise or judgment. Regardless of what we call it, we all experience the observing ego's presence.

I prefer the perspective that I own my observing ego; it is part of me and I can change its rules based on God's truth through the power of the Holy Spirit. This begs the question, however, "What are these rules and how did they get into my mind?"

Our observing ego has no rules when we are born. It develops throughout our life based on input from significant people such as parents, caregivers, friends, a spouse or an ex-spouse, and others such as teachers and coaches. They give us the rules for what is right or wrong for us to think, and what is appropriate for us to do. Our observing ego uses these rules to determine if we are good or bad, and if our behavior is appropriate or not. The health of our observing ego and its rationale is influenced heavily by the mental, emotional, and spiritual health of the significant individuals from whom we receive our rules.

A reliable parent can teach a child that he or she can make mistakes and not be a bad person, and that he or she can be forgiven and the relationship restored. A mean and angry parent can tell a child that he or she is fundamentally bad for various reasons, or perhaps even no reason at all. Unfortunately, the child's observing ego will dutifully add this rule to the others as though it is true. Left unchallenged, this rule will remain as truth from that point on. A rule can also be missing. If a child does not experience forgiveness by a parent or caregiver, he or she has no reason to include a rule that God or anyone else will be forgiving.

Implanting life-giving rules or injecting those that are toxic happens easily with children because they are naïve and believe what they are told. This is why Scripture and what God says about us are the most important sources of rules that we intentionally acquire to replace those that are unreliable.

Georgeann and I use our observing egos when we interact with each other. We are aware of our emotions, and watch for attitudes that can arise from the activation of previous wounds. We know each other's wounds, and are aware of our option to either be gentle and merciful, or harsh and condemning. We can either lovingly speak words of healing into those wounds, or savagely thrust our verbal sword into them.

We are also aware of how each other is responding by facial expressions and body language. We ask ourselves if *the other is understanding* what we are saying. And, we ask ourselves if *we are understanding* what the other is saying. Of even more importance, each of us ask ourselves if *we* are understanding what *we* are saying. In this way, we are engaged in the interaction both as a participant and as an observer. We also use our observing egos in exactly the same way when we are working with others.

When you get furious with Jack during an argument, your observing ego is very close to being shut down and of minimal value in helping you know if you are understanding him, or if he is understanding you, or if you are understanding why you are angry. A response is always better than a reaction. People often get furious with someone in an instant and have no idea why. We will cover this in a future email, but for now I can tell you that it usually has to do with re-opening a childhood wound.

A condemning observing ego

Recall that a healthy observing ego lets us know when we have done something right or wrong. If we realize we did something wrong, we can ask for forgiveness and make amends. However, if the rules of our observing ego are only condemning, its conclusions are flawed. We will condemn ourselves for anything we do for any reason or no reason at all. We will always believe that what we did wasn't good enough, or done soon enough, or not whatever enough. According to this type of unhealthy observing ego, no matter what we do, we are bad and deserving of punishment and rejection. These relentless harsh judgments can result in a constant sense of guilt, badness, and shame.

Narcissists

Narcissists, in contrast to having a condemning observing ego, have a different type of unhealthy observing ego that has no room for guilt or badness and the resulting shame. Their observing ego is completely comfortable spewing blame and shame on anyone else for anything and everything that does not turn out exactly as desired. People who accept this blame from narcissists become shame bearers. They end up feeling bad about themselves because they are wearing the narcissist's shame, which has nothing to do with their own. By the way, narcissists do not keep people around who do not accept this shame transfer, and who insist on holding them accountable for their words and actions. If you refuse to bear their shame, you will be discarded like a used tissue.

The following is the part that might sound like heresy.

Trying to confess inappropriate shame

When you try to confess inappropriate shame to God, meaning that which was spewed onto you from someone else, it is very difficult for you to *experience* God's forgiveness. The reason is that you can only claim the *real blood* of Jesus for your own *real sin*, not the *imagined sin* that has been shamed onto you from someone else, or even inappropriately from yourself.

For example, people cannot confess and receive forgiveness for being "condemning and judgmental," if the basis for their belief is they were told they were by a condemning and judgmental person. It is much more likely that their accuser is projecting his or her own condemning and judgmental character onto them.

What makes people vulnerable to receiving this type of inappropriate shame is that, at times, the vast majority of us can be condemning and judgmental. If you combine this truth with a desire to be humble and authentic with God, and then add the convincing sincerity of an accuser, you end up with a person who experiences a non-resolving sense of self-condemnation and self-judgment for thinking they are condemning and judgmental. These feelings of inappropriate shame are not from God.

I'm not saying that the blood of Jesus cannot heal and deliver you from anything and everything; because it can. But, I repeat, His *real blood* is meant to provide you with *real forgiveness* for your *real sins*, not the *imagined sins* that have been inappropriately shamed onto you from someone else, or even inappropriately from yourself. If you are experiencing someone else's shame, what you need is not forgiveness, rather, you need a renewing of your mind such that you do not receive their shame in the first place.

Renewing your mind

> Therefore, I urge you, brothers and sisters, in view of God's mercy, to offer your bodies as a living sacrifice, holy and pleasing to God—this is your true and proper worship. ²Do not conform to the pattern of this world, but be transformed by the renewing of your mind. Then you will be able to test and approve what God's will is—his good, pleasing and perfect will. (Romans 12:1-2)

You need to offer yourself as a living sacrifice to God for the renewing of your mind, not offer yourself to someone else for its continued distortion by accepting their shame. It is only by offering yourself to God that you will be able to test and approve what His will is by His rules, and not succumb to the will of others by their rules. This renewal is to *no longer accept* the inappropriate shame of others, or the toxic rules that were injected into you by unreliable rule-providers. This is why seeking forgiveness for inappropriate shame does not result in the experience of change and true freedom. Change and true freedom in this type of situation only occurs with a renewing of your mind that is no longer vulnerable to receiving and believing the inappropriate shame of others. When someone tries to project inappropriate shame onto you, you can either think the timid and submissive thought of "Well, this person might be right. I should apologize," or the bold and authoritative thought of, "No, this person is wrong! I refuse to receive anyone's shame!"

Healthy narcissism

Just to be complete, I should point out that there is healthy narcissism in that if you do something well, it is fine for you to experience satisfaction in your accomplishment as long as when you do not do something well you also accept and take responsibility for the outcome. God has no problem with anyone enjoying their accomplishments and finding satisfaction in their work or other activities, as long as those accomplishments and that satisfaction do not displace Him. Humility is not the absence of healthy narcissism, it is praising God and giving Him the glory in the midst of it.

The health of an observing ego is on a continuum

I should also mention that an observing ego is not either healthy or not, and that its health can vary depending on the area of life. Its ability to function reliably in each area is on a continuum between healthy and unhealthy. These areas include work, recreation, ministry, marriage, parenting, etc.

For example, we may function well at work knowing what our coworkers, subordinates, or superiors need, only to come home and be insensitive and demanding with our family. Or, we may be extremely effective at home with our spouse and children, yet go to work and participate in gossip and backbiting. God wants our observing ego to grow in all areas of our life. To this end, we are constantly adding, refining, or removing rules through experience, insight, and power of the Holy Spirit. Growth in one area usually helps you make progress in the others.

Once our observing ego has rules that are healthy enough and reliable enough to be useful, we can use it to develop skills for interacting with others based on its observations. This means that when you and Jack are arguing, you can participate and observe the argument without becoming immersed and losing your perspective. You can look for ways that one or both of you may be contributing to the argument without either of you being wrong and deserving of blame and shame. You can remain creative and thoughtful in ways to deescalate the argument back to the original conflict that can be no more than a misalignment of perspectives. You can remember what helps each of you understand the other, and what does not. Try to be authentically engaged without fear of rejection and abandonment.

As you and Jack develop healthier observing egos, your arguments will decrease in frequency and intensity. You will have the ability to identify your previous wounds and current issues, along with the courage to accept them as your own. I promise.

I will write more on love, respect, and needs in my next email.

In Him,

Rick

P.S. Caroline, this is Georgeann,

Hormones

Rick and I read each other's emails to you and Jack before we send them. I pointed out a glaring omission in this one about what can also have a major impact on a woman's observing ego - hormones! He said, "You're right. I need coffee. You write this part."

Over the years hormones have tried to have a significant influence on me. It doesn't matter if it is PMS, pregnancy, or menopause. I always tried to accept them as a very real part of being a woman, and not let them control my life. Obviously, that's easier said than done. Hormones come and go, and there's no sense fighting them or condemning yourself for how they make you feel. And, there's no reason to allow anyone else to condemn you either. I was always honest with my family if it was a particularly bad month.

One time when our first daughter was about six years old, I heard her greet Rick at the door. She said in a hushed voice, "Dad, be careful. Mom is P H S ing. He replied softly, "Don't you mean P M S ing. She paused and said, "Yeah, that's it." Rick and I learned to take my hormones, as well as his, seriously.

Delivering two children took a toll on my body that resulted in negative self-talk. One time after taking a shower I was standing in front of our full-length mirror when Rick walked into the room. He saw the look on my face and asked, "Are you wondering where some of your beauty went?" I nodded. He said, "Stay right there." He came back and held our sleeping eight week-old daughter next to my reflection in the mirror and said, "Here it is."

Over the years our bodies have changed, and what remains is that we are still God's gift to each other. I am his place of joy and he is mine. For forty-three years we have kept our physical expression of love for each other alive and evolving. He has said to others, "Some things on Georgeann aren't exactly where I first met them, but I can still find them." And, he keeps me wanting to be found.

Caroline, this is Rick again.

What she said. ☺

Subject: Re: Your Observing Ego and Shame

Georgeann, this is Caroline.

Thank you for your story about the mirror. It helps to hear the truth. Jack has always been supportive in that regard. He's also very understanding of my hormone swings. His mother taught him a lot about women.

Rick,

What you wrote about an unhealthy observing ego makes sense. I also liked the offering myself as a living sacrifice. Though, I am more often like a squirming sacrifice trying to get off the altar.

I have always struggled with feelings of self-criticism, condemnation, and shame. Some mornings I wake up feeling guilty when there is nothing to be guilty about. I often blame Jack for being critical of me, but to be honest, I am far worse on myself.

When I described my family I was a bit misleading. My family has not always been so happy and warm in expressing emotions.

My parents did not get saved until I was starting high school. Before that, there was a lot of arguing and fighting. They are amazing people now, but back then it was pretty tough. I remember lying in bed at night hearing them argue and wishing there was something I could do to make them stop. One night when I was in grade school I faked being sick and it worked. They stopped, but started up again a couple nights later.

Now I can look back with more clarity and realize how frustrated they were not knowing how to love each other, us kids, or even themselves. They were completely lost. They never apologized, but it doesn't matter because I have forgiven them and thankfully it is all in the past. Their love for us is unquestioned.

I need to give more thought to narcissists. I am pretty sure I have encountered a few. Jack isn't one because he is willing to admit his mistakes...at least most of the time...eventually. ☺

Caroline

Subject: Re: Re: Your Observing Ego and Shame

Caroline, this is Rick.

There is no *too late* with God

It isn't uncommon for parents to find Jesus and turn their lives around when their children are older. I think it is the years of struggle that finally compel them to look for another answer. The problem is that if their children were teenagers or young adults at the time, they have already developed most of the rules for their observing ego along with automatic instincts for survival. One young adult in this situation told me, "It's great for them, but too late for me!" I responded, "There is no too late with God. Psalm 51:10-12 has been encouraging to me throughout my spiritual walk.

> Create in me a pure heart, O God,
>   and renew a steadfast spirit within me.
> 11 Do not cast me from your presence
>   or take your Holy Spirit from me.
> 12 Restore to me the joy of your salvation
>   and grant me a willing spirit, to sustain me.

I know of very few parents who woke up each morning wondering, "How can I mess up my kids even more today?" It is more likely that parents cannot give what they never received and do not have. Everyone progresses through various stages of growth that, unfortunately, do not occur soon enough for some relationships, especially those with their children.

Apologizing to others

We have all made mistakes in our relationships, and if there is a path to peace and reconciliation, it begins with accepting responsibility, offering an apology, and trying really hard not to do it again. And, if we want forgiveness and mercy from those we have offended, we also must give forgiveness and mercy to those who have offended us.

When apologizing to someone, asking for forgiveness can pose a bit of a problem. It can be perceived as wanting even more from the person who was wronged. Forgiveness should be a *freewill gift* from the person who was wronged, not words that he or she is *compelled* to speak to make the offender feel better. One approach that I use is to say, "If you can forgive me I would appreciate it, and if you cannot, I understand." If someone is unwilling to forgive me, I have no choice but to release it to the Holy Spirit.

Sufficient grace from God

Ultimately, when it comes to sins and offenses toward others, we need to find the same *sufficient grace* from God for ourselves that was sufficient for the Apostle Paul when he wrote in 2 Corinthians 12:9 about his request for the Lord to take away a "thorn in the flesh." The Lord's response and Paul's conclusion was,

> "'My grace is sufficient for you, for my power is made perfect in weakness.' Therefore I will boast all the more gladly about my weaknesses, so that Christ's power may rest on me."

I'm not to the point of boasting about my weaknesses, but I am more honest about them.

Issues from the past can continue to be expressed

You wrote about your parents in your last email that, "…I have forgiven them and thankfully, it is all in the past. Their love for us is unquestioned." Unfortunately, half of that is not true. I have no doubt that your parents love you. The problem is that some of the issues your family had in the past are not only "in the past," because some continue to influence you in the present. These issues continue to express themselves through the same broken rules and behaviors that you now need to offer to God for the renewing of your mind. This takes time and is why we need to be intentional with God about asking for forgiveness and continually offering ourselves to Him as a living sacrifice. Life is a long and difficult journey with no shortcuts or easy solutions. Even so, I can't think of anything better to do with the time we are given.

In Him,

Rick

Subject: Re: Arguing, Needs, Love, and Respect

Warning: This is another one of those long emails.

Caroline, this is Rick.

I hope our last couple of emails on the observing ego were helpful. The very mention of the word "ego" can throw some Christians into a tailspin. I see it as just a name for an aspect of how God created us that helps us interact with one another.

People have reasons for their thoughts and actions

Back to one of your previous emails. Georgeann and I are not in the habit of telling people they are "wrong" because people have reasons for their thoughts and actions, even when, in many cases, those thoughts and actions are self-destructive and/or hurt others. Our assumption is that people do whatever makes sense to them. This even applies to people with mental illness or a personality disorder. If we do not understand why someone does something, we assume that we do not have or understand *enough* of the pieces to their puzzle. I use the word "enough" because no one has or understands all of the pieces to anyone's puzzle, including their own.

We rely on the Holy Spirit to reveal what needs to be changed, along with when and why. It is God who helps people want to change and empowers them to do so as Paul states in Philippians.

> Therefore, my dear friends, as you have always obeyed—not only in my presence, but now much more in my absence—continue to work out your salvation with fear and trembling, [13] for it is God who works in you to will and to act in order to fulfill his good purpose. (Philippians 2:12-13)

That said, when a couple is not living according to God's wisdom, we are not shy about helping them understand the consequences of their beliefs and actions to themselves and others.

Then truth and now truth

A key concept we help couples understand is the difference between *then truth* and *now truth*. For example, when growing up it is possible that no one cared what a child thought or needed, but now, a spouse does. The childhood rule, "No one cares what I think or need" would be a *then truth* and not a *now truth*. However, if he or she does not accept the new *now truth* and continues to think and act like no one cares, including their spouse, their relationship with their spouse and others will suffer.

The reverse can also be true in that during childhood, people cared what a child thought and needed, and he or she assumes that the *then truth* of others caring is also a *now truth* for a spouse who does not. It is essential for couples to create a *now truth* that is based as much as possible on evidence of love, hopeful assumptions, and fulfilled godly desires and needs.

Both husbands and wives need love and respect

I am familiar with Ephesians 5:33 that you mentioned, and the teaching of some authors that emerges from it that women need love and men need respect. To be honest, I find that assertion to be true, yet insufficient. Can you imagine Jack gently pulling you close to him and whispering, "Caroline, I love you so much, but I don't respect you." Or if at dinner you gazed at Jack and said, "Honey, I really respect you, but I don't love you."

Georgeann and I have found that husbands and wives have the same areas of need, whether they will admit it or not. Both need acceptance, a sense of belonging, affirmation by others, etc., but not to the same extent or intensity. Those who believe they do not need these, and claim they are just fine without them, are very likely to be well-defended against their pain from not having them met previously and sufficiently by others. This idea of a wife and a husband having the same areas of need to a varying extent and intensity also makes sense in that both are being conformed to their unique image of the same Jesus.

Desirable traits of a wife or husband

A long time ago I wrote the following paragraph describing what I desired in a wife.

> I desire a peaceful, steady, and consistent wife who listens to my dreams, and believes in me. Someone who is willing to hear God equally for the two of us, and has the courage to speak the truth in love when I have lost my perspective. I need a wife who is strong, gentle, and confident that God will provide for us as we work together in our ministry. I need a wife who knows me and loves me in the midst of my struggles and failures, as well as my efforts and successes. I need a wife to share it all, and celebrate the achievements with me, and mourn the losses. My wife needs to be a partner who seeks neither to dominate me nor make me her idol.

I haven't met anyone who would prefer the opposite as follows.

> I desire an angry, chaotic, and inconsistent wife who refuses to listen to my dreams, and continually doubts me. I want someone who is willing to hear only her desires, and has the aggression to speak her criticisms when I have lost my perspective. I need a wife who is vacillating, hostile, and convinced that I am the only one who provides for us. I need a wife who does not know me and condemns me in the midst of my struggles and failures, as well as minimizes my efforts and successes. I need a wife to keep all that she wants, and who only enjoys the achievements with me, while blaming me for the losses. My wife needs to be a person who dominates me and makes me her idol when it suits her to get what she wants.

Now let's try the positive version for a husband that Georgeann would desire.

> I desire a peaceful, steady, consistent husband who listens to my dreams and believes in me. Someone who is willing to hear God equally for the two of us, and

has the courage to speak the truth in love when I have lost my perspective. I need a husband who is strong, gentle, and confident that God will provide for us as we work together in our ministry. I need a husband who knows me and loves me in the midst of my struggles and failures, as well as my efforts and successes. I need a husband to share it all, and celebrate the achievements with me, and mourn the losses. My husband needs to be a partner who seeks neither to dominate me nor make me his idol.

And, here is the opposite.

I desire an angry, chaotic, and inconsistent husband who refuses to listen to my dreams, and continually doubts me. I want someone who is willing to hear only his desires, and has the aggression to speak his criticisms when I have lost my perspective. I need a husband who is vacillating, hostile, and convinced that I am the only one who provides for us. I need a husband who does not know me and condemns me in the midst of my struggles and failures, as well as minimizes my efforts and successes. I need a husband to keep all that he wants, and who only enjoys the achievements with me, while blaming me for the losses. My husband needs to be a person who dominates me and makes me his idol when it suits him to get what he wants.

In the interests of full disclosure, is Georgeann like my positive description of a wife all the time? No. Am I like my positive description of a husband all the time? No. Have we both been growing in that direction over the last forty-three years through the grace and mercy of God in the power of the Holy Spirit? Absolutely!

Do not ignore your needs

When you wrote, "As far as my daily needs are concerned, it is wrong for me to be preoccupied with them," we could not agree more. We do not advocate a preoccupation with your needs, though, your needs should not be ignored either.

The New International Version of Philippians 2:3-4 says,

> Do nothing out of selfish ambition or vain conceit. Rather, in humility value others above yourselves, ⁴not looking to your own interests but each of you to the interests of the others.

We prefer the English Standard Version (ESV) of Philippians 2:4 where it says, "Let each of you look not only to his own interests, but also to the interests of others." The "not only" is important to note. When Paul was encouraging his readers to look to the interests of others in verse 4, he was contrasting it to the motives of "selfish ambition or vain conceit" in verse 3. Paul was not advocating a selfless denial of personal needs. Whichever translation you prefer, if your own needs remain unmet indefinitely, you eventually will not be able to meet any of the needs of others.

Another reason to be sensitive to your needs is that it is difficult to hear the Holy Spirit for others and give wise counsel when you are empty and exhausted. This does not mean that the Holy Spirit cannot work through you when you are empty and exhausted, but that should not be your typical condition.

Our best example of someone tending to personal needs and taking time for rest and prayer is Jesus who, "…often withdrew to lonely places and prayed" (Luke 5:16). And, if Jesus' example is not compelling enough, even a dog with a litter of puppies knows enough to get up, shake them off when necessary, get some food and water, and take a needed stroll in the backyard. And how those puppies (and people) will howl. I'm not sure exactly what they say, but it falls along the lines of, "How could you leave us?" "We're all going to die!" "You are selfish and don't care about us!" Or, "You are only thinking of yourself!" At first these accusations and demands may cause her concern, but eventually she learns that everything will be fine as long as she takes care of herself enough to have something left to give.

You also mention Acts 20:35 about it being, "...more blessed to give than to receive." That doesn't mean that it is not blessed to receive, just more so to give. ☺

I agree with what you wrote about storing up treasures in heaven by giving to others, though we also should let those very same others give to us in our need so their storehouses will be filled as well. You see, people who are not willing to receive, deny others the joy of giving, and people who are always giving, deny others the opportunity to grow in that area. That is but one reason why we need to be honest with ourselves and others about our needs.

Healthy relationships are give and receive

Some people say that healthy relationships are "give and take." I prefer the phrase "give and receive," in that one person gives and the other receives what is offered. People who "take" from a relationship, often end up taking more than what the giver was willing to give, even though the giver may not resist. This type of relationship is more characteristic of fleas and intestinal parasites robbing life from a dog or cat.

Christians often struggle with how much to give of themselves. The balance is to give only what is intended and intend only what is not debilitating. Anything beyond that results in feelings of being drained and abused. This can only occur with someone's permission, their naïveté, or perhaps a willingness or psychological need to be abused. While I am not saying how much you should give in any particular relationship, I am saying that what you give needs to be intentional for it to be a gift.

Abuse in the area of giving and receiving can be a reenactment of childhood wounds for those whose desires and needs were not acknowledged, affirmed, and met by parents, caregivers, family members, or peers. For many of these children, acceptance required unconditional submission and servitude, and the complete suppression of their desires and needs. Their broken rule for *give and receive* relationships was *give and only give*.

Unfortunately, some children react in the opposite manner and become takers without regard for anyone else's desires or needs.

Their childhood rule is, "The world owes me whatever I want whenever I want it." Both the complete suppression of personal needs by one spouse, or the selfish demand that all desires be met by the other are toxic to a marriage relationship.

I am a bit concerned that you are so uncomfortable focusing on yourself to the point that you "hate it." Beth had to work through similar feelings that her desires and needs were not important. She felt it was because of your older brother Tim. Your reasons may be completely different, but Beth felt like he was causing the family enough pain and that anything she wanted was just that much more of an added burden. Her *then truth* is not her *now truth*. Even then, it wasn't true that her desires and needs were not important to your parents, but the logic of a child makes sense at a child level. "I love my parents. My parents are sad. My needs will make them even sadder. I will keep my needs to myself. I have no needs."

Jesus often calls others to meet our needs

It is good that you trust Jesus to meet your needs, though it is dangerous to look only to Him when He is calling someone near you to meet your needs as part of His will. He has called Jack to meet your needs as your husband. He has called you to meet Jack's needs as his wife. I don't want to seem harsh, but when Jack said you could not have him and walked out of the room, you wrote, "I have never felt so alone." If I may ask with all humility, where was Jesus? If you had Jesus with you, and Jesus is all you need, why did you feel so alone?

My point is that Jesus is there to help us endure our tragedies and pain, but he rarely makes it as though they never happened. That night you needed Jack, not Jesus, to comfort you, affirm your needs, and talk about ways to restore your closeness. Jack is the one who Jesus called to meet your needs in that moment, and he failed. The good man that Jack is, however, refused to let that failure stand.

We all fail each other at various times. I have failed Georgeann far more often than I thought I would. The important question is, what comes after our inevitable failures? The answer for us is healing and growth. Our healing and growth through marriage only occurs when, as a couple, we address the real causes of our conflicts, which more often than not are rooted in our desires, needs, fears, wounds, defenses, and assumptions.

Self-love

One last thought concerning needs. We believe our first and foremost need from ourselves is self-love. Nothing good comes from self-loathing or self-condemnation. Our belief is based on Jesus' answer when he was asked, which is the greatest commandment in the Law.

> Hearing that Jesus had silenced the Sadducees, the Pharisees got together. 35 One of them, an expert in the law, tested him with this question: 36 "Teacher, which is the greatest commandment in the Law?"
>
> 37 Jesus replied: "'Love the Lord your God with all your heart and with all your soul and with all your mind.' 38 This is the first and greatest commandment. 39 And the second is like it: 'Love your neighbor as yourself.' 40 All the Law and the Prophets hang on these two commandments." (Matthew 22:34-40)

In this passage Jesus explicitly gives us not only permission to love ourselves, but he makes it an *imperative* in order to fulfill the second commandment which is to "Love your neighbor as yourself."

This does bring up the question, however, how can we offer a genuine love to our neighbors that we do not give to ourselves? There is a big difference between acting loving and being loving.

Self-love requires a genuine *non-condemning* and *non-condoning* belief system of not condemning our humanness, and not condoning our failures.

I have to be honest about my self-love. I am sure my neighbor would not appreciate the level of condemnation and judgment that I often have towards myself.

That confessed, everyone experiences the discrepancy between what they want to do, compared to what they end up doing. The Apostle Paul expressed it clearly in Romans 7:15. " I do not understand what I do. For what I want to do I do not do, but what I hate I do."

The same principle of self-love is true for needs. How can we genuinely provide for the needs of our neighbors if we ignore our own? Your needs should matter to you because they matter to Jesus. They are guides not only for your healing and growth, but Jack's as well as he grows in his ability to respond to you.

Jesus does not reject us because of our needs the way others often do. It is when we accept our needs that we more fully and authentically accept ourselves, along with who we are in the body of Christ, and the promise of who God will enable us to become. We all need to receive and experience the grace and mercy that Jesus suffered, died, and was resurrected to give us.

In Him,

Rick

Subject: Boundaries and Needs

Rick, this is Caroline.

I originally thought your working with Beth for a year would be ideal for me, and perhaps it will be. The problem I am realizing is that you think you know more about my experiences than I have told you. The result is you popped up in an area of my head where I did not invite you. Tim is off limits.

Beth and I have very different experiences with Tim and he isn't someone I want to talk about. If you can't respect that, then we are finished. I'm sure this doesn't sound courageous like your other couples, but it's just the way it is. I hope you aren't offended by my first paragraph, but as you can see, I did not erase it.

I have given more thought and prayer to the possibility that talking with Jack about my desires and needs could be helpful to our marriage. After all, Jack is smart, but he isn't a mind reader. It just feels so uncomfortable. I don't want to be a burden to him and I don't want him to feel bad or inadequate. He is an amazing man and I'm completely blessed to be married to him.

I have several questions about my desires and needs.

How do I know if they are justified? How would I know if I am only being selfish? What if I have a desire that is in conflict with Jack's?

I always want more *us time* with him, and he doesn't have enough time to give me all I want. That certainly isn't fair to him. I will continue to pray about it.

I did have insight on the idea of *then truth* versus *now truth*. It isn't only a childhood/adulthood issue. It can be a this minute/next minute experience such as when I accepted Jesus as my Savior. Before my decision, I was not saved, and in the next instant I was. That immediate change in truth didn't feel uncomfortable at all. I guess it proves that I am able to accept a radically new *now truth*.

Respectfully,

Caroline

Subject: Re: Boundaries and Needs

Caroline, this is Rick.

Thank you for letting me know that I crossed your boundary. Please let me know immediately if I do it again in another area. Georgeann and I consider your life and marriage to be sacred ground onto which it is our privilege to be your guests. It is never our intent to cause you or Jack unnecessary pain. Your concern that you don't "sound courageous" could not be further from the truth. It takes great courage to set and maintain healthy boundaries in any relationship.

Speaking the truth in love

As to your desires and needs, you won't know if they are justified or selfish until you become fully aware and embrace them. You must examine them in light of Scripture and God's wisdom before you can make a valid assessment. Unfortunately, the wisdom people often use to examine themselves is not wisdom from God, rather, it is their own wisdom and rules that emerged as a result of childhood wounds. This kind of wisdom is often driven by fears of being re-wounded or rejected.

For example, if a very small boy who comments on the prickly nature of the whiskers on his grandmother's chin as she presses them into his tummy and chest during play is met with a stern look, and the end of an otherwise enjoyable time together, he will learn that speaking the truth to someone you love leads to rejection. It doesn't take too many repetitions of similar events to solidify the rule, *Do not tell the truth if there is a chance it will hurt someone's feelings because you will be rejected.*

Now, fast forward to when that same child is an adult and needs to be truthful for the health of his marriage and the spiritual growth of his spouse. That unchallenged rule, *do not tell the truth,* will get in the way of what he wants even more. It isn't that the rule is never true, it's just that applying it consistently by never being honest with his spouse out of the fear of being rejected is not helpful.

Though the Apostle Paul does not mention our internal rules explicitly, he touches on this idea in the context of reaching our fullness in Christ and "speaking the truth in love." In Ephesians Chapter 4: 14-16 he writes,

> [14] so that we may no longer be children, tossed to and fro by the waves and carried about by every wind of doctrine, by human cunning, by craftiness in deceitful schemes. [15] Rather, speaking the truth in love, we are to grow up in every way into him who is the head, into Christ, [16] from whom the whole body, joined and held together by every joint with which it is equipped, when each part is working properly, makes the body grow so that it builds itself up in love.

Paul finishes this passage with "…makes the body grow so that it builds itself up in love." This means that speaking the truth in love and wanting to hear the truth is not only essential for healing and growth in a mutually satisfying marriage, it is also essential for the healthy functioning of the Body of Christ.

Us time

In your email, you wrote that you wanted more *us time* with Jack. There are three types of *us time* found in this passage from Ephesians. The first is your *us time* with Jesus as you "grow up in every way into him who is the head, into Christ." We need to be more intentional in seeking and leaning into our *us time* with Him.

The second type of *us time* is what you have with others as His body that is "joined and held together by every joint with which it is equipped, when each part is working properly." This means that we as Christians need meaningful *us time* together because we are functioning partners in Christ.

The third *us time* is an extension of the second for Christians who, in addition to being members of His body, are also partners in a marriage relationship. Your desire for more *us time* with Jack is not only a need for you, Jack, and your family, it is also a need for the Body of Christ as the two of you serve individually and together.

Georgeann and I are functioning partners in our marriage, family and the Body of Christ. For our partnership to be successful, we need to have meaningful *us time*. Otherwise, we are merely associated roommates with each of us having our respective tasks. In essence, relationships like this are parallel lives of functional convenience where "speaking the truth in love" is not valued, rather, the best that is hoped for is "speaking the facts efficiently." I'm not saying that speaking facts efficiently is not important for a healthy marriage, it's just a poor substitute for intimacy.

Returning to your desire for more *us time* with Jack and your concern about being fair to him because he is so busy. Your assumption is that Jack does not need as much *us time* as you do. In fact, Jack may be completely unaware of his need for more *us time* with you. Just because he has gotten by with less than you desire, it doesn't mean he hasn't always needed more in order to become more and more content and conformed to the image of Jesus. What better way is there for Jack to grow in this area than for God to have him marry someone whose desire and need will draw him into it? It is Jacks commitment to become the husband God wants him to be that will cause him to persevere in this growth.

Family strengths and weaknesses

As I alluded to earlier, children usually adapt to their family's strengths and weaknesses by forming rules and behaviors for either thriving or surviving. This means that a family may have a strong sense of integrity and work ethic without a sense of empathy for others. Another family may be sensitive to the needs of others and have a dim view of those who are driven by success and finances. God's ideal is a combination of both sets of strengths. He wants mature Christians who have integrity and a strong work ethic, are sensitive to others, and are good stewards of their personal abilities and finances so they can invest effectively in His kingdom.

Growing in each other's strengths

Ideally, spouses bring the strengths of their family of origin to their marriage, and use their marriage relationship to heal and grow in their weaknesses. From what you have shared about Jack's family showing very little affection, it is no surprise that he would need help growing in this area. Please do not think I am being critical of Jack's family because every family has its strengths and weaknesses. I'm sure you can think of Jack's strengths into which you can grow in order to be more fully conformed to your unique image of Jesus.

The best path for couples to grow in each other's strengths is to intentionally, faithfully, and courageously speak the truth in love for the mental, emotional, spiritual, and physical health of each other and their relationship. The result is that both people benefit from the process, even though it may require conflict before there is resolution and growth.

Georgeann and I believe that a mismatch of strengths with the opportunity for healing and growth in weaknesses is one of God's purposes for the well-established phenomenon, "Opposites attract."

In Him,

Rick

Subject: Opposites attract

Rick and Georgeann, this is Caroline.

Opposites attract!!!! Are you kidding me?!!!!

Jack and I are opposites in everything! He is athletic, I'm not. He likes spicy foods, I don't. I go to bed early, he stays up late. I am flexible, he is rigid. I am lenient with the kids, he is strict. I am spontaneous, he is a planner. When buying things, I am happy to pay for quality. Jack wants quality at the very lowest price, and I mean the very lowest. I am often embarrassed by his haggling. I connect to people emotionally, he connects intellectually. I like romance comedies, he likes action adventure. When we argue, he has to be right, especially when he is not. I tell him what I feel, and he tells me what he thinks.

One time on a walk I pointed out a beautiful butterfly to him. Do you want to know his response? He said, "I wonder how it stays in the air with the shifting breezes and still gets to where it wants to go?" Really Jack?!?

J-Dear, I know you are reading this and you know it is true. I can think of one thing besides ministry that we really agree on, and that is why we have two children. ☺ I love you Babe, but we are most definitely opposites.

So Rick and Georgeann, how do we overcome this? I'm crazy for him, and made crazy by him. Now I'm really frustrated.

Caroline

Subject: Re: Opposites Attract

Caroline, this is Georgeann.

I could not stop laughing when I read your email because we have lived through the same trials of being opposites.

Rick and I are very different. In fact, early in our marriage Rick was a lot like how you described Jack, and I was a lot like you. One difference is that I thought I was not very intelligent and Rick was extremely so. I have since learned that I am intelligent and he is extremely so in some areas…but not all. I know how frustrated you are, and I will offer you a different perspective that helps us do less arguing and be more appreciative of how unique we are from each other.

Attraction of opposites is for healing and growth

Since God's will for you is to be conformed to your unique image of Jesus, he uses many types of relationships in your life to help bring that about. The most intense, productive, and potentially destructive relationship is marriage. We believe that one of God's purposes for the attraction of opposites is for their healing and growth, not their continual irritation of each other.

Everyone emerges from their family of origin with areas of strength and other areas that are not fully developed. Some areas may even be wounded and deformed. When two people of opposite strengths first find each other, they often feel like a whole human being because an area of weakness in one is covered by a strength of the other. Obviously, this is not always true, but the tendency is well established.

While identifying and maintaining complementary strengths is ideal in a business partnership, God wants a couple to grow in each other's strengths so both will be more fully conformed to the image of Jesus. This means that a strength in one spouse serves as a model for the other to observe and build into his or her own character. Unfortunately, this is not always how spouses respond. Sometimes spouses react to the other's strengths with criticism and dismissal. They view God's provision with contempt.

Recall from a previous email that one spouse's desires and needs often represent areas in which God wants the other to grow. And, it is by this growth that those desires and needs can be fulfilled. In the same way, one spouse's strength can make the other more aware of a weakness. Realizing that a weakness exists and that growth needs to occur can be humbling. And, the actual growth itself can be painful.

For example, when one spouse who is able to connect emotionally tries to build a relationship with the other who is not, the other starts feeling uncomfortable. This discomfort identifies the underdeveloped area in which that spouse needs to grow and possibly heal. This healing and growth only occurs, however, if both people know what is causing their discomfort, want to heal and grow, are committed to overcoming the pain, and know what to do.

The first step each day in achieving healing and growth is no doubt familiar to you and Jack by now. It is in Romans 12:1-2 where the Apostle Paul urges that we offer ourselves to God as a living sacrifice for the renewing of our mind.

> Therefore, I urge you, brothers and sisters, in view of God's mercy, to offer your bodies as a living sacrifice, holy and pleasing to God—this is your true and proper worship. 2 Do not conform to the pattern of this world, but be transformed by the renewing of your mind. Then you will be able to test and approve what God's will is—his good, pleasing and perfect will.

A more complete expression of God's character

Another purpose for the attraction of you and Jack as opposites has everything to do with Billy and Erica. Jack's strengths are his unique expression of God's character, and your strengths are your unique expression of God as well. When the two of you honor each other's strengths, as opposed to competing for whose are superior, Billy and Erica will see a combined expression of God's character that is more complete than what is possible by either of you individually.

Based on what you wrote about yours and Jack's strengths, Billy and Erica will learn from the two of you when and how to be flexible or rigid, lenient or stern, or how to be a spontaneous planner. They can learn how to be shrewd or generous when bargaining, and how to connect emotionally and intellectually. They can learn how to explore their feelings and thoughts when communicating with others, or even when disagreeing or arguing with their spouse. As for spicy food and watching romance comedies or action adventures, they will have to figure that out on their own. ☺

Competing strengths and justified weaknesses

Unfortunately, many couples do not choose the path of blended strengths, healing, and growth. Each insists on defending their incomplete expression of God's character along with justifying their weaknesses. We have often heard the statement, "That's just the way I was made." This begs two questions, "Made by whom, God or man?" and "Are you as fully conformed to the image of Jesus as God wants you to be?"

Some spouses insist on criticizing their partner's differing strengths as being inferior because it is much easier to criticize and devalue someone's strengths than to grow in them. What their children see is an ongoing battle between childish adults who insist on defending their strengths and justifying their weaknesses. This leaves children in the position of having to decide who is right and who is wrong, and which character traits are valuable and which are not. These children have no choice but to choose because they are in the process of building their own character and observing ego with its own set of rules and approved behaviors. And, they will choose from what they see.

Traits that attracted can become irritating

When couples do not honor each other's strengths, the very traits that were attractive when dating, become irritating when married. The boyfriend who beamed when he saw his girlfriend walk into the room becomes the husband who doesn't even look up. The girlfriend who was a joy to hold during a movie, becomes a wife who gets in the way of her husband's laptop while he is working and the movie is playing in the background. Then again, she will eventually learn to occupy herself on her phone. The girlfriend who was a joy to walk with, becomes a wife who won't stop talking during a walk because she is starved for the attention she used to get when they were dating. Everything that was new and exciting becomes common and mundane.

What I just wrote is the devastating path of destruction that married couples stumble down unless they remain as intentional about building a mutually satisfying marriage as they were about pursuing each other when dating. Of course, if when dating, one or both were not intentional, or did not share the same commitment to be conformed to the image of Jesus, they will have an extremely difficult time building a mutually satisfying marriage. I am completely confident that you and Jack do not fall into this category. If you did, you would not have reached out to us for help, and continued exchanging this many emails.

Let me know what thoughts this brings to mind, especially the part about honoring each other's opposite strengths.

Blessings,

Georgeann

Subject: Re: Re: Opposites Attract

Georgeann, this is Caroline.

You're saying the oppositeness that we have been fighting over for as long as we have been together is actually God-preferred? He wanted us to begin our marriage that way? He designed it that way? That my image as a representation of Jesus is different from Jack's, and we are both just fine?

I have tried all my life to conform to others in order to fit in and win their approval, and you are telling me that was completely unnecessary? That my opposite strengths in relationships with others is God's design? I don't know whether to be relieved or angry! I bet your response is I can be both. Right?

All this time, Jack and I have been arguing over who should be in control. Everything must be either my way or Jacks, rather than knowing when it should be his strength or my strength. And, we should be growing in each other's strengths. We talked about this last night and he is interested in what this could mean.

Ok, I started this email last night, and this morning we had another argument. I don't know what I should do.

Jack was talking about a meeting later in the day with our ministry team, the area director, and a member of the advisory council from back home. They were going to talk about establishing and ranking our priorities, and based on that, look at our budget. I decided to do what you said.

I listened for a while and finally pointed out that this would be a great time for him to practice relying less on his strengths of planning and budgeting, and to grow in my strengths of being more trusting and flexible. He looked at me like I was a total idiot. I can't remember all he said, but the gist of it was that this meeting was far too important for that, and I wouldn't understand. He said it was easy for me to "sit back and pray while he did all of the work."

Jack, I'm sorry for upsetting you. Feel free to correct me if I am wrong about what you said. To your credit, you didn't yell at me this time, but once again, it feels like we are worlds apart.

Georgeann, now what? I just want to stop trying because it doesn't seem to do any good.

Caroline

Subject: Fix or Facilitate

Caroline, this is Georgeann.

I changed the subject line to *Fix or Facilitate* because we have shifted away from Opposites Attract.

First, you have nothing to be sorry about. You tried to help Jack with the upcoming meeting and it didn't work. If we had a dollar for every time we fell into this type of argument, we could pay to fly to where you are…and live there for a year!!!

The problem with your last disagreement is we haven't had time to give you and Jack tools for dealing with that type of situation.

Jack, as you read what I write to Caroline about how she could have helped you better, I want you to think about ways you can help her when the circumstances are reversed. The questions you should ask her will be similar.

Answer Mode

For a short time after we were first married I would come to Rick to talk about a problem or difficult situation, and he would immediately go into Answer Mode. The format was something like, "Well, what you need to do is blah blah blah blah blah." He may as well have tacked onto the end of it, "And you are such an idiot. You should have come up with this very simple solution on your own."

Even when his suggested answer was correct, it didn't help me understand my feelings about the situation, or grow into becoming a better problem-solver. It also did not help me become more and more conformed to the image of Jesus, or to be a more effective member of the Body of Christ.

Be genuinely curious

Rather than try to fix my problem with an answer, Rick's role is to help facilitate me in understanding what I think and feel. He does this by becoming genuinely curious about my situation and asking me questions. These questions follow the pattern of Who, What, When, Where, Why, and How much? Be careful about asking "Why" questions such as "Why did you do that?" People often do not have a readily available and accurate answer to that one. Of course for these questions to be helpful, a spouse needs to be willing to honestly explore his or her thoughts and feelings, and the questions cannot sound like they are coming from a prosecuting attorney.

Over the years Rick and I have become very good at asking these questions, which has allowed us to build trust and confidence in each other. We trust that the other has our best interests in mind, and we are confident that the other will speak the truth and ask questions in love.

The purpose of asking questions is to help the other person disentangle jumbled thoughts and surface underlying feelings such as, fear, frustration, anxiety, or anger. Questions include:

What options are you considering? (For each option that is being considered ask the following questions.)

What do you like about it?

What do you not like about it?

What are the potential gains? How likely are they?

What are the potential losses? How likely are they?

How do you feel about this option? When have you felt this way before?

Do you have enough information to make a decision? If not, is there anyone you can contact who does?

Is there any way I can help?

When each question is answered, it is good to follow up with, "If I understand you correctly, you are saying <repeat back>." This allows the other person to hear their thoughts coming back from someone else, which usually results in greater clarity. Sometimes it is helpful to follow up an answer with, "Is there more to that?" This gives the other person a chance to explore the possibility that there could be deeper thoughts and feelings to consider.

Asking questions and repeating back will seem mechanical at first and perhaps even contrived, which is fine. It is important to remember that all change in behavior is clumsy at first. When Rick and I are doing this for each other we know exactly how the other is trying to help, and have learned to appreciate and cooperate with the effort.

Questions not to ask are:

Why haven't you tried <add your solution here>?

Why have you waited until now?

What do you expect me to do?

How did you get into this?

What were you thinking?

Why does this always happen to you?

These questions are, more often than not, no more than statements of condemnation, shame, and guilt hurled at someone who is already hurting. It isn't that these questions should never be asked, it's just a matter of when the timing is right, and how they can be asked in a more effective form that will result in productive answers, healing, and growth.

Helpful alternatives to the previous questions are:

Are there other solutions you have thought of?

What time pressures are you under?

What can I do to be helpful?

What unforeseen events contributed to this problem?

What logic led you to make that decision?

What do you think is contributing to this pattern?

Questions that might have helped Jack gain clarity on his thoughts and feelings about the upcoming meeting are:

I know we have talked a lot about this, but what are your priorities for our ministry?

How would you rank our priorities if you had to?

What are your thoughts about the budget?

Do you think our director and the council member will be open to your ideas? If not, how will you respond?

Do you have any reason to doubt their sincerity?

As I just wrote, when appropriate remember to follow up an answer with, "Is there more to that?"

Then you end with something like:

I believe in you and trust that God will be with you. You have a good heart and I will be praying for you and everyone at the meeting.

The two of you must avoid any opportunity to become polarized defenders of two mutually exclusive positions. For example, if you asked,

"Do you have any reason to doubt their sincerity?" and Jack replied,

"Yes, they only care about how much money is being spent!"

Do not attempt to offset or balance his view by saying,

"That's unfair. They are sacrificing a lot to be here."

That is when the discussion would likely escalate to,

"Sacrifice! Are you kidding me? I'm the one out here doing the work and they get to sit back in their air conditioned homes and judge me! Do they think they can come out here for three lousy days and understand what I am going through? No way! And why are you siding with them?!"

Then you are obligated to respond,

"I'm not siding with them! I just want you to look at this realistically! What have they ever done to make you think this?!!!

A better response to his statement about their concern only being about the money spent would be the honest and non-threatening question,

"What has led you to think that of them?"

Jack might have a perfectly good reason for his suspicions about the director and the council member's sincerity and concerns about the budget, or his suspicions may be completely unfounded. What is critical is that you help Jack explore his thoughts and feelings. It may be that Jack is the one consumed with the budget and he is projecting what is true about himself onto them.

Jack, I am only using this as an example. I have no idea what you think or don't think about budgets and the motives of others.

We are often asked if we do this helpful questioning with each other all the time. Not always. Sometimes one of us will have to say in the middle of a discussion, "Wait a minute, I'm not looking for an answer. I just need help thinking this through." Occasionally one of us will even start a discussion with the statement, "I need to talk about something and I am not looking for an answer…yet."

Learning to facilitate each other's thinking and problem-solving is a skill that takes practice. You must be patient with, and encouraging to, each other. Your first goal should not be to *convince* Jack about your thoughts and feelings, rather, it should be to help him *understand* his own. Afterwards, he may be more willing for you to speak y*our truth in love* into his life.

Your truth in love

I write y*our truth in love* because no one has the whole truth and nothing but the truth. I have my truth from my perspective and Rick has his. The only *true truth* is God's from His perspective. In everything Rick and I are both incorrect to some degree. What is always true, however, is to let love and respect prevail.

All patterns from the past are not bad

It is clear that both of you are committed to building a mutually satisfying marriage, and are struggling with what to say or do to avoid previous patterns of conflict. All patterns from your past are not bad. Think back to when you were dating and first married. Do you remember what each of you would say and do that was appreciated by the other? It is fine to return to those words and actions as a beginning point for restoring and renewing your relationship.

Take care,

Georgeann

Subject: Re: Fix or Facilitate

Georgeann and Rick, this is Caroline.

Feel free to fly here whenever you want. Once you get to the airport, the three-day bus ride isn't too bad. After that, the two-day boat ride upriver can be a bit dicey. For the rest of the way we'll make sure you get two of our best donkeys. Drop by any time.☺

Jack's meeting went well. They will be here for two more days. We actually found time last night to talk and he has some thoughts on marriage as a partnership and opposites being attracted to each other. It may be a few days before he has time to email you.

We have printed out the questions from your last email on how to facilitate each other's thinking and put them on our refrigerator. Actually, they should be mounted on the wall in a box with a glass front that says, "Break in case of emergency."

My schedule is pretty tight for the next few days. I lead three women's Bible studies and have a lot to prepare. Billy hurt his ribs climbing a tree, or I should say falling out of a tree...again. Even though he is half monkey, it's his human part that falls! I'm going to use that as an object lesson for one of the studies on how our best efforts do not always turn out as we hope.

Take care,

Caroline

Subject: Re: Arguing, Needs, Love, and Respect

Hello Rick and Georgeann, this is Jack.

I apologize for not getting back to you sooner. I had to make an emergency visit to one of our sister churches. The worship leader and the guitar player had an argument that escalated into an all out shouting match in front of the worship team. They were actually throwing things. When we met, they got into it again. I kid you not, they sounded like two children.

It always amazes me how things pile up when I am gone. I know you are very busy and we appreciate you spending your time to work with us.

I must say that you three have covered a lot of ground in my absence. It nearly wore me out just going through the emails.

Your exchange about love and respect with me telling Caroline that I loved her, but did not respect her cracked me up. It does make me think about what we have been taught on submission in that same chapter.

You wrote about having a partnership marriage with Georgeann, yet Ephesians describes a relationship of submission when it reads,

> Wives, submit yourselves to your own husbands as you do to the Lord. 23 For the husband is the head of the wife as Christ is the head of the church, his body, of which he is the Savior. 24 Now as the church submits to Christ, so also wives should submit to their husbands in everything. (Ephesians 5:22-24)

The Apostle Paul also writes in 1 Corinthians,

> 34 the women should keep silent in the churches. For they are not permitted to speak, but should be in submission, as the Law also says. 35 If there is anything they desire to learn, let them ask their husbands at home. For it is shameful for a woman to speak in church. (1 Corinthians 14:34-35)

This does not describe a marriage based on partnership.

Thoughts?

I'm late for a meeting. I'll write more later.

Best,

Jack

Subject: Pre-Fall Marriage

Jack, this is Rick.

It is good to have you back. It's never pleasant confronting people who refuse to get along. Arguments and backbiting can siphon an enormous amount of energy away from a ministry or family.

Spending time or investing in others

I'm sure you recall from a previous email that Georgeann and I look closely at the words people use. We aren't "spending" time with you and Caroline. We are *investing* our lives in you the same way others have invested in us. Our return on investment is the two of you having a great marriage that you and your children enjoy, and one that your children internalize and pass on to their children. This vision becomes reality when, as we wrote earlier about Romans 12:1-2, we offer ourselves to God as a living sacrifice.

> Therefore, I urge you, brothers and sisters, in view of God's mercy, to offer your bodies as a living sacrifice, holy and pleasing to God—this is your true and proper worship. ² Do not conform to the pattern of this world, but be transformed by the renewing of your mind. Then you will be able to test and approve what God's will is—his good, pleasing and perfect will.

Recall what we wrote about how people can either *go to* God's altar to pray, or *climb up onto* His altar and offer themselves to Him as a *living* sacrifice. Offering yourself is what pleases God and allows Him to not only address the ways you have become conformed to this world, but also to transform you by the renewing of your mind. "Then you will be able to test and approve what God's will is—his good, pleasing and perfect will." God also does not want you *working for Him*, rather, He wants to *work through you*. I keep bringing this up because I often need reminding. It is so easy to fall back into my own effort. When writing these emails I am often reminded by the Holy Spirit that He wants to speak and work through me, not for me to speak and work on my own. Though He does need me to type. ☺

First century Roman culture model of marriage

So what is God's good, pleasing, and perfect will for your marriage? I do not think a reenactment of first century Roman culture is a suitable model because it emerged from a period in our Christian history when wives were considered to be the property of their husband.

Of course there are still many men, and fewer women, who think it is fine for a wife to submit to her husband in everything, and be silent until she is instructed on what to think and do. When it comes to 1 Corinthians 14:34, "the women should keep silent in the churches...", according to this, the wisdom of the most qualified woman is inferior to that of the least qualified man.

Proverbs 31 model of marriage

Another model for marriage is at the end of the Book of Proverbs.

Epilogue: The Wife of Noble Character

10 A wife of noble character who can find?
    She is worth far more than rubies.
11 Her husband has full confidence in her
    and lacks nothing of value.
12 She brings him good, not harm,
    all the days of her life.
13 She selects wool and flax
    and works with eager hands.
14 She is like the merchant ships,
    bringing her food from afar.
15 She gets up while it is still night;
    she provides food for her family
    and portions for her female servants.
16 She considers a field and buys it;
    out of her earnings she plants a vineyard.
17 She sets about her work vigorously;
    her arms are strong for her tasks.
18 She sees that her trading is profitable,
    and her lamp does not go out at night.
19 In her hand she holds the distaff

and grasps the spindle with her fingers.

20 She opens her arms to the poor
and extends her hands to the needy.

21 When it snows, she has no fear for her household;
for all of them are clothed in scarlet.

22 She makes coverings for her bed;
she is clothed in fine linen and purple.

23 Her husband is respected at the city gate,
where he takes his seat among the elders of the land.

24 She makes linen garments and sells them,
and supplies the merchants with sashes.

25 She is clothed with strength and dignity;
she can laugh at the days to come.

26 She speaks with wisdom,
and faithful instruction is on her tongue.

27 She watches over the affairs of her household
and does not eat the bread of idleness.

28 Her children arise and call her blessed;
her husband also, and he praises her:

29 "Many women do noble things,
but you surpass them all."

30 Charm is deceptive, and beauty is fleeting;
but a woman who fears the Lord is to be praised.

31 Honor her for all that her hands have done,
and let her works bring her praise at the city gate.

This woman does it all to the point that, "Her husband is respected at the city gate, where he takes his seat among the elders of the land." (verse 23) I am not sure in what ways she was submitted to him or silent, but his job of being a husband appears to have been pretty easy given her initiative and effectiveness.

Pre-Fall model of marriage

Georgeann and I prefer a Pre-Fall model of marriage that was God's original will for Adam and Eve before the Fall when they were banished from the Garden of Eden. I first heard of this perspective during a presentation by Steve and Katie Helgeson at Harvest Vineyard Church in Ames, Iowa. When they finished, I was torn between two responses. The first was to sit there stunned and think, "Why have I never heard this before?" The second was to get up and start throwing chairs across the room yelling, "Why have I never heard this before?!!!"

I'll begin my explanation of a Pre-Fall Marriage with Jesus.

In the Sermon on the Mount Jesus taught what has become known as the Lord's Prayer.

> "This, then, is how you should pray:
>
> "'Our Father in heaven, hallowed be your name,
> 10 your kingdom come, your will be done,
>   on earth as it is in heaven.
> 11 Give us today our daily bread.
> 12 And forgive us our debts,
>   as we also have forgiven our debtors.
> 13 And lead us not into temptation,
>   but deliver us from the evil one.' (Matthew 6:9-13)

When Jesus said, "your will be done on earth as it is in heaven" we think He meant it literally. So, what is God's will for how marriage should be done on earth? As I just wrote, the obvious answer to us is in the way He created Adam and Eve to be together before the Fall.

Before the Fall, in the first account of creation God said,

> 26 ..."Let us make mankind in our image, in our likeness, so that they may rule over the fish in the sea and the birds in the sky, over the livestock and all the wild animals, and over all the creatures that move along the ground." 27 So God created mankind in his own image, in the image of God he created them; male and female he created them.
>
> 28 God blessed them and said to them, "Be fruitful and increase in number; fill the earth and subdue it. Rule over the fish in the sea and the birds in the sky and over every living creature that moves on the ground."

²⁹ Then God said, "I give you every seed-bearing plant on the face of the whole earth and every tree that has fruit with seed in it. They will be yours for food. ³⁰ And to all the beasts of the earth and all the birds in the sky and all the creatures that move along the ground — everything that has the breath of life in it — I give every green plant for food." And it was so.

³¹ God saw all that he had made, and it was very good. And there was evening, and there was morning — the sixth day. (Genesis 1:26-31)

This section begins with, "Let us make mankind in our image, in our likeness so that they may rule..." This gives me a sense of the beauty, love, and power that was built into "mankind" as the image of the "us" who were present at creation.

God's purpose for mankind was to "rule over the fish in the sea and the birds in the sky, over the livestock and all the wild animals, and over all the creatures that move along the ground." The question is, who is this "mankind" that is supposed to rule? Verse 27 says, "So God created mankind in his own image, in the image of God he created them; male and female he created them."

There is no indication that God's original will was for males to *rule over* the animals, and females to not do the same. And, there is certainly no indication that God originally intended males to rule over females. When God said, "...so that they may rule over..." He made them coequal ruling partners without a hierarchy or a distinction of dominance. This means that Adam and Eve were originally created to be complementary to each other. Together, in their oneness, they ruled and reflected a greater fullness and representation of God than either was created to be individually.

In the second account of creation in Genesis Chapter 2:18 God said, "It is not good for the man to be alone. I will make a helper suitable for him." This means that Adam was lonely, and evidently, God was not enough. Therefore, God created Eve to make Adam complete, which I also believe made Eve complete with Adam. This brings me to the idea of "helper."

Eve was not *originally* created to be Adam's assistant, and once again, the notion of Adam ruling over her only surfaces after their fall in Genesis 3:16 when God was speaking to them. '"To the woman he said, "I will make your pains in childbearing very severe; with painful labor you will give birth to children. Your desire will be for your husband, and he will rule over you."'

I've been confronted with the question, "What about what the Law says about marriage?" or the statement, "We live in a fallen world, husbands rule over their wives, and that's just how it is."

First, Jesus fulfills the law as written in Matthew 5:17. "Do not think that I have come to abolish the Law or the Prophets; I have not come to abolish them but to fulfill them."

And second, as far as a fallen world is concerned, even though we as Christians live *in it,* we are not *of it.* Therefore, if we who are married are to bring about God's will on the earth as it is in heaven, our marriages are the best place to start.

I am well aware that even considering this notion of a coequal husband and wife marriage can cause some Christians to develop a nose bleed. In fact, some husbands really like the idea of ruling over their wife. These one-sided relationships are particularly endemic with Christian abusive husbands whose entire *Own Testament* consists of a single corrupted verse,

> "Wives, submit yourselves to your husbands. The wife
> does not have authority over her own body, but yields
> it to her husband. Do not deprive each other. And, if
> she divorces her husband and marries another man,
> she commits adultery." (All About Me 1:1)

For a man who opts for a Post-Fall marriage, I recommend the Proverbs 31 woman over a wife who is aligned with first century Roman culture because it will require a lot less work on his part. Proverbs 31 does start, however, with the question, "A wife of noble character who can find?"

For the man who does find a Proverbs 31 wife, he would do well to appreciate, encourage, and praise her, rather than criticize, discourage, and condemn, which often happens when his ego feels dwarfed by her excellence. When it comes to caring for a Proverbs 31 wife, we can learn at least one lesson from a dairy farmer. No matter how angry he gets, he is smart enough not to kick his best cow in the udder.

Jack, when you get a chance, I would still like to know your thoughts about spinning plates.

In Him,

Rick

Subject: Pre-Fall Marriage and Opposites Attract

Rick and Georgeann, this is Jack.

The Pre-Fall model of marriage is completely new to me. Don't get me wrong, it makes sense. I like the idea that Caroline and I are coequal partners because that's the way we've been functioning. She has her areas of responsibilities and I have mine. But what about when we can't agree and a decision has to be made?

I also get that opposites attract, and I agree with Caroline that it can be irritating. What irritates me even more, though, is that I never knew it was God at work in us and through us. Even so, things have changed between us.

I remember when we first met that Caroline was a breath of fresh air. She was upbeat and carefree. I just felt different about life when I was with her. I actually felt different about myself as well. She accepted me as I was and she believed in me. What made her completely unique in my life was that when she praised me, there wasn't a big "but" attached to it. "But you could have done …", or "But you forgot to… " or "It would have been perfect, but you…". I wanted to be with her as much as I could.

Now it seems like nothing is good enough. When she questions me I feel attacked like I'm some incompetent fool. She says that isn't what she means, though that's exactly how it feels. And when she is mad, she pulls herself inward and acts like I'm not even in the room. I had enough of that growing up. Why would I want to try to connect and get more of the same?

Since Caroline is going to read this anyhow, I'll take a risk and let her read it before I click Send. I know she will see this differently and we may as well deal with things as efficiently as possible.

Really Jack?! You want efficiency?

Connect when?! When do you have time to connect? You come home late, you eat, you acknowledge the kids, and then you go to your desk in the side room to work. Connection can't be all that bad because you do so little of it!

When you do pay attention to me I know what is coming next. It isn't that I mind being intimate with you, I actually enjoy it, but why is it you only approach me when it is for sex? Sometimes I just want to be held. When do you check in with me to see if I just need to talk? You often tell me you don't have enough time to talk. If you have enough time to argue, you have enough time to talk!

Nice point about us having our areas of responsibility. I have a full schedule keeping our household running, being a mother, homeschooling our children, and ministering to the women in the village. They tell me very difficult things, and I am tired of carrying everything alone.

I also want to be the wife for you that God intended me to be. When we were dating we would talk for hours about God and life and our struggles with faith and family. I could share my insecurities and dreams for the future. We were real with each other. You were safe. Now we just talk in passing to synchronize our schedules. Granted, you do maintain our home to perfection. Unfortunately, it's a perfection that I can't keep up with.

Am I one of those plates that Rick wrote about? If so, I don't think I ask for all that much spinning from you. I do a pretty good job of spinning on my own. At times, YOU are the plate that I have to keep spinning so YOU won't fall.

We never had these kinds of problems until we got here. Or, if we did, there were enough distractions to hide them. I'm alone here. I left three of the closest girlfriends I will ever have just to come here. I need you now more than ever. This is not the way it was supposed to be. Feel free to carry on with your email to Rick and Georgeann.

This is Jack.

I was wondering when we would get real with you. This is much more what our evenings are like. I'm tired. I'll maybe write more in the morning.

Good morning, this is Jack again.

We talked last night. It didn't start out very well. I challenged her on her statement that I only approach her when I want sex because it just flat out isn't true. I approach her in a positive way all the time for things not related to sex. Once she finally agreed, we talked about many things that were bothering us.

I have been goal oriented and a hard driver all of my life. I was All-State in football, wrestling, and baseball. I compete to win at everything. If anyone beats me they earned it. I chose not to play sports in college because there was no way I could go pro.

To be absolutely honest, I thought Caroline's love and acceptance when we were dating was because she had me up on a pedestal. I always feared that when she finally found out who I really was, she would not love me. She knows a lot more about me now than she ever did, and she says she still does.

I've got meetings all day and will be leaving tomorrow morning on an overnighter. This feels like the worst possible time to be gone. I don't know what to do about our marriage. I really have no idea what I should do. The last thing I ever thought I would fail at was marriage. I would trade every accomplishment I have ever achieved for a great marriage.

Jack

Subject: Good News

Rick and Georgeann, this is Caroline.

I know you haven't had time to respond to yesterday's bombshell email, but I had to let you know what Jack did. Tonight, just before supper, Billy's friend from next door brought me an envelope. Jack had given it to his mother this morning before he left. I'm sure he gave it to her because he didn't want me to find it until after he was gone. I'm always up when he leaves on a trip so I can send him off with a blessing.

The note inside said, "I love you very much and we will work through this together. Please don't give up on me." It just melted me. Leaving me notes is what he did when we were dating in high school. He would push them through one of the vent openings in my locker.

I have no idea how all of this will end up or how difficult our journey will be. I have been praying and claiming Romans 8: 9-11.

> You, however, are not in the realm of the flesh but are in the realm of the Spirit, if indeed the Spirit of God lives in you. And if anyone does not have the Spirit of Christ, they do not belong to Christ. 10 But if Christ is in you, then even though your body is subject to death because of sin, the Spirit gives life because of righteousness. 11 And if the Spirit of him who raised Jesus from the dead is living in you, he who raised Christ from the dead will also give life to your mortal bodies because of his Spirit who lives in you.

If God can raise Jesus from the dead, He can raise us and our marriage to the life we were meant to have.

I feel bad about dumping so much on the two of you in our last email, but as painful as it was, I have a peace about it.

Caroline

Subject: Re: Good News

Caroline, this is Rick.

Georgeann is mentoring a young woman this morning, picking up our granddaughter after school, and will go out to the barn to look in on her horse. She won't be back until late tonight, so I will write you. She will be glad to hear about the note Jack gave you.

Your subject for this email is an understatement. It is more than "Good News," it is Great News! Building a great marriage requires intentionality from both partners. The message in notes like Jack's is, "I was thinking loving thoughts about you even when you weren't with me." That's a great way to make you feel special and cared for. Great job Jack!

Please don't worry about "dumping so much" on us. We've worked with a few couples who were so hesitant about opening up, they were like someone going to a dermatologist and during the examination insisting on wearing a snowsuit, boots, gloves, and a hat. Others, on the other hand, are completely open from the start. The bottom line is that people are ready when they are ready. There is no single "right" way for couples to do this kind of work.

I'm going to wait a few days to respond to the "efficiency" email from you and Jack because I want the two of you to read it together when he gets back.

Helping other couples

In the meantime, I know we haven't written specifically about how you and Jack could add a marriage-related ministry to what you are doing, but most couples we work with want to help others in the same way they have been helped.

If you find yourself helping other couples it is critical to understand that it takes time for them to trust you enough to feel safe and let you into their deeper thoughts and feelings. It also takes time for spouses to build the same trust and safety with each other.

There will always be a mismatch between spouses regarding the speed and depth that they want to go when addressing their desires, needs, fears, wounds, defenses and assumptions. What matters is how great the mismatch is and in what areas. The real problem is when spouses do not want to go to the same depth, nor talk about the same issues.

An illustration of this is when a couple on vacation by the ocean agrees to meet at a dock to go diving. The wife is waiting with rented scuba gear, and the husband arrives with a snorkel, mask, and fins. It is unlikely that the wife will be fulfilled by the dive if she can only go as deep as her snorkeling husband. Then again, using a snorkel may be the best her husband can do for awhile, and once the peace and joy of snorkeling are experienced, he may be willing to rent scuba gear to go deeper.

Building a healthy marriage takes time and practice, and as I just wrote, a willingness for spouses to trust each other as they work their way into their deeper issues. Couples who are successful, patiently respect each other's process for healing and growth. When both are sincere, time is on their side.

It really isn't that difficult to help couples who are serious and want to work at building a great marriage. Of course, people who are struggling with mental illness, a personality disorder, or require medication to function will need to have help from professionals such as a licensed counselor, physician, or a psychiatrist. There should be no shame in these circumstances because people need what they need. That said, if you think you may be in over your head when working with a couple, then you probably already are.

Remember, everything we write in these emails applies to couples, not to spouses in an abusive relationship. In an abusive relationship, the dominating person almost always does not want to be honest, while the other does. Unfortunately, what can happen is that the spouse who is being abused feels safe when meeting with you and Jack, and may be brutally honest. While this is happening, the abuser may act passive and accommodating only to be brutal on the drive home and the days that follow. The sad fact is that you can only help a couple if both spouses want your help. That said, the tremendous truth is that for those couples you can help, your impact on their lives, and the lives of their children and others will last for generations.

Not trying to scare you, but there just aren't enough trained counselors to meet the needs of all of the couples who are struggling. Laypeople must help whenever they can. All of us can learn from one another.

Blessings to you both and safe travel for Jack,

Rick

Subject: Imago, Romance, Power Struggle, and a Conscious Marriage

Jack and Caroline, this is Rick.

Decision-making

We often get the question about which of us decides on a course of action if we can't agree. For us, in forty-three years, it has not happened. We keep praying, listening, and talking until we come up with a plan we can agree upon. Sometimes the agreement is a conscious submission to the other. In essence it is, "I don't want to do this, but I will agree to do it together." This means that once we commit, we try not to express resistance, reluctance, second guessing, back-biting, or bitterness. Notice I wrote, "try not to express" those things.

We are still human and have the right to feel what we feel, and sometimes things just pop out. That said, if the decision that was agreed upon does not turn out well, we do not persecute the other person for being wrong. The main reason is that what we say or do usually comes back to us in the future. If grace and mercy are given, they will likely be received in return. This is consistent with the old adage, "What goes around comes around."

What goes around comes around

One time when Georgeann backed out of our garage, she didn't notice our other car in the driveway to her left. She ended up scraping half the length of both cars. In her defense, she had just started taking a new allergy medication. I heard the scraping from inside and came running. When I got there, she was getting out of the passenger side and was furious with herself. I put my arms around her and assured her it could have happened to anyone.

About four months later I was slowly driving our Blazer to our mechanic's garage and she was following in our other car. I had a portable battery pack under the hood and did not get the hood latched. All of a sudden the hood flew up, bent the hinges, and cracked the windshield. When I got stopped, I looked in the side mirror and saw her walking towards me. I was really glad that I had been supportive about her accident, because she was bringing to me the same grace and mercy I had brought to her.

Three phases of a marriage relationship

What I am about to write is heavily influenced by the work of Drs. Harville Hendrix and Helen LaKelly Hunt. Their thinking, and our own, is much more expansive and nuanced than what I can include in this email, so please bear in mind that what follows is an oversimplification of both. I will present three phases of the marriage relationship from Harville and Helen's work, though we are giving thought to other phases that couples may go through.

Romance phase

Jack, in your previous email, the "breath of fresh air" that you attributed to Caroline when you first met and were dating occurs during the romance phase. This phase has so little to do with reality it could be referred to as psychosis. Any quest for reality during this phase is hindered because both people tend to hide their undesirable traits and pretend to be the ideal match. Couples in this phase tend to ignore or not perceive the warning signs.

Imago

So, how do we recognize who we think is our ideal match? According to Harville and Helen, during childhood we build a subconscious image in our mind of the person who will be the ideal nurturing other. They refer to this as the Imago, and it is built from the previous relationships and behaviors of our parents, caregivers, siblings, or any other people who were influential in our life; pleasant and not so.

When someone comes along who subconsciously triggers a match with our Imago, we think the long-awaited caregiver has finally arrived who will meet all desires and needs, and will be safe and playful. Conversely, the other person is also watching for the same type of match with his or her Imago.

A young woman who is treated with respect by her father or other influential person will likely be attracted to someone who does the same if her Imago was formed around the value of respect.

Unfortunately, if she was treated with disrespect, she may be attracted to the same kind of relationship because it feels familiar. And it is familiar because her Imago and personality were formed around that disrespectful attitude and behavior.

We have often heard couples say, "When we first met we felt like we had known each other forever." Guess what? They had, just in different people. Of course, this doesn't describe all relationships. Sometimes the exact opposite occurs in that anyone who would treat the woman I just mentioned with the slightest disrespect, would be dismissed instantly and lucky to be allowed to live.

Everyone's Imago is not always overtly driven to find someone to fulfill their own specific desires and needs. A person may be totally content with solely focusing on the other's desires and needs without the slightest concern for his or her own. When this happens, the relationship is likely mimicking one they had in their family in which someone else was the constant focus of attention for reasons that were either good or bad. In that case, the Imago is programmed to seek out a similar person and follow the same pattern of pretending to have no desires or needs, and becoming invisible in the relationship. In essence, the paradoxical desire and need is to maintain the appearance of having no desires or needs. One reason for this can be that the psychological pain of having desires or needs that remain unmet, is more painful than pretending to have no desires or needs at all...at least for a while.

Opposites attract

A person who had nurturing parents will likely be attracted to someone who is the same. The confounder is when the *opposites attract* kicks in. An example is when someone who is a nurturer is attracted to a person who is a self-centered narcissist that is a bottomless pit of never ending demands. Or, someone who is sensitive and values communication is attracted to another who is rarely aware of his or her feelings and is barely verbal.

It would take dozens of books and therapists to fully flesh out these patterns and their complexities. You will have to forgive my attempt to raise your awareness in a single email.

Power struggle

Once the near-psychotic-mist of the romance phase clears, couples are left with the reality of what was always there in the other person, and in themselves; just not perceived. This is when the power struggle phase begins in which one or both spouses shift from appearing to have no needs and being desirable, to focusing on getting their needs and desires met. In addition, agendas that were hidden from each other are brought to the surface.

Tactics of the power struggle can range from pleading and passive-aggressiveness to mental, emotional, spiritual, and even physical abuse. Some spouses think screaming, pouting, or hitting will convince the other to become more nurturing, safer, playful, and more available to fulfill his or her desires and needs. These strategies are often used unsuccessfully by small children.

During the power struggle phase, feelings of not getting what was bargained for can start up in both spouses. At the core of their perceived rip off, however, is the fact that they both actually fell in love with their own fabricated image, their Imago of the ideal match that they projected onto their future spouse. Many of the traits they thought they perceived were not there at all. It is like projecting a movie onto a screen and thinking the images on the screen are truly part of the screen. In addition, negative traits that were missed become clearly visible. Sadly, these negative traits in one's spouse were often seen clearly by family and friends before the marriage.

Some rip offs are not merely perceived. These intentional deceptions by a spouse during the romance phase, which was no more than hunting for a spouse by a hunter, were calculated and then revealed without shame after getting married. These hunters are content with the power struggle because they have no intention of building a mutually satisfying marriage. They think a marriage certificate is the same as a car title. Once received, the holder of the title can legally do with the other person whatever he or she pleases because "God hates divorce." Recall the first century Roman culture ownership model of marriage.

Conscious marriage

Couples who make it through the power struggle enter into what Harville and Helen refer to as a conscious marriage. The alternatives are to remain in the power struggle indefinitely, or divorce and find another person with whom to go through yet another romance phase followed by the obligatory power struggle. This cycle of dead-end new beginnings can be endless; especially when someone is addicted to the hopes and emotions of the romance phase.

In a conscious marriage, spouses become intentional in what they say and do. This means they are not destined to react towards each other with prefabricated defenses that protect childhood wounds and soothe longstanding fears. Rather, they become more intentional in responding to each other in ways that promote understanding, healing, and growth. That said, decades of instinctive reactions are very difficult to overcome, and subduing them completely takes slightly longer than a lifetime. However, the battle of transforming our instinctive reactions into intentional responses is a power struggle that God desires for us to enter into by first offering ourselves to Him as a living sacrifice. He is the one who renews our mind and conforms us to the image of his Son.

Jack, the fact that it was so important for Caroline to accept you and believe in you without a "but" attached to it, and now you feel attacked and like an incompetent fool, leads me to believe that you have some childhood wounds around acceptance and competence.

It is clear to me that you feel safe and nurtured by Caroline when the two of you are in sync with each other. That is why it hurts so much when she pulls inward and withdraws. Often it is our inner-child who responds with contentment when someone accepts and encourages us, and can be that same inner-child who reacts with anger and rage when we are rejected or ignored.

Sadly, some people are so wounded in the areas of rejection and neglect that they are numb and no longer feel the pain. This does not mean the pain is not present and does not impact their mind, emotions, spirit, and body; it just means it is no longer perceived.

It is good that you and Caroline experience pain when you withdraw from each other because it helps motivate you to get back together. The tragedy is when a couple is in more pain when together than when apart because they have no clue about how to deal with each other's desires, needs, fears, wounds, defenses, and assumptions. One or both spouses may be too fatigued or simply unwilling to do so.

A common defense against experiencing the pain of abandonment and loneliness is to convert it to anger or even rage. The reason often is that experiencing anger is much more tolerable than feeling vulnerable and abandoned.

Caroline, your angst about your need for closer connection with Jack makes perfect sense in light of how you and your family are connected. Connection is a required nutrient in your emotional diet. It sounds to me like you are the *Connector in Chief* in your relationship with Jack. What I mean is, it sounds like you are the pursuer; the one who usually closes the gap. This means Jack, more often than not, is the receiver of your pursuits.

Jack, if this is true, don't expect Caroline to continue to do most of the heavy lifting in this area. Remember how you pursued her when you were dating and in the romance phase? The pursuing of each other that makes for happy dating and romance is also required for a happy and romantic mutually satisfying marriage.

Caroline's loss of close fellowship with three of her girlfriends makes it even more critical for you to connect deeply with her. Even though she agreed and wanted to go on this tour, the loss of regular contact with her girlfriends still created a void. I am sure at the time the two of you made the decision, she did not fully appreciate the extent of her upcoming sacrifice. The good news is that she still needs and wants connection with you, and this tour is an opportunity for the two of you to grow even closer.

Jack and Caroline,

When spouses fail to establish the connection of a conscious marriage, we have seen many instances where they fulfill their marriage relationship needs by diverting them towards children, friends, work, or even a ministry. It's not that these other relationships should not be pursued, but problems occur when they become substitutes for a marriage relationship. When this happens, spouses usually end up living parallel lives, and their marriage often ends when their last child leaves home.

Of course, another substitute is other lovers. These relationships often begin with a mental and emotional connection that leads to a romance phase with its addictive psychosis. When that psychosis clears, however, a another diversion is usually found to take its place.

On a much happier note, even though the romance phase of your relationship has ended, God's will is that the two of you transition as quickly as possible through the power struggle to a conscious marriage. It is in your conscious marriage that you will heal and grow with a much deeper and more abiding passion for romance, wholeness, and oneness than was possible in the romance phase. The struggles you are going through now are an unavoidable part of your journey to a mutually satisfying marriage. God's perfect path is often painful.

I need to stop here because tonight is our weekly date night and I still have to get ready. I will write more later.

In Him,

Rick

P.S. If you are interested in learning more about Harville and Helen's work, we recommend the book, *Getting the Love You Want: A Guide for Couples* by Harville Hendrix, along with their communication initiative called, *Safe Conversations*.

Subject: Areas of Responsibility and Physical Intimacy

Jack and Caroline, this is Rick.

We just got back from a wonderful date. Dinner and an evening stroll in a neighborhood that we haven't walked in before.

Areas of responsibility

I will pick up where I left off with some thoughts about your separate areas of responsibility. It is fine to be responsible for an area, but not always good if you must deal with it alone. It is important to keep each other informed and to ask for input when needed. We know of several situations where a husband who was taking care of the finances died unexpectedly and his wife was clueless about what to do next.

When spouses share decision-making, they are using their combined gifts that God has given them. If one does not understand something and wants to, it is incumbent upon the other to teach it to him or her. I'm not saying that spouses should not function in the area of their strengths, though sometimes they are not as strong in an area as they think.

When we were first married I informed Georgeann that I was head of my household and I would be handling the money. She replied that she was good at that sort of thing. I repeated myself and after more discussion she reluctantly said, "Okay." One month later we were two months behind! I have no idea how it happened and was fairly sure it wasn't even possible. I went to her and said that I was still head of my household and I would like to delegate to her the responsibility for handling the money. She smiled graciously and said, "I would be glad to." She won an argument that did not happen by being patient and letting circumstances unfold. I was a young man who could never have been convinced of the lesson that I quickly learned.

Only, never, and always

Next, I will address Caroline's comment about when you do pursue her it is "*only* for sex," and the disagreement that followed when the two of you tried to talk about it. Words like *only, never,* and *always* can be distracting when you are trying to grow closer. It is easy to get sidetracked with comebacks such as "Only? You mean I *never* approach you for any other reason than for sex?! *Ever*?" It isn't about whether or not *only*, *never*, or *always* are always true; it just feels that way when those words are used. It is more helpful to look past those words in an effort to understand what the other person is feeling and trying to say.

Jack, I am sure you pursue Caroline in ways that are not only for sex, but it sounds like she wants other and more frequent pursuits as well. This brings me to the topic of physical intimacy.

Physical intimacy

Physical intimacy does not have to be orgasm-focused. Bob and Beth learned that for them, physical intimacy begins with a gentle touch or an affectionate pat on the leg. Beth relaxes and feels connected with Bob when they sit next to each other on the porch, or when he gives her a foot rub with hand lotion and has no expectations of her for himself. They discovered that this type of intimacy resulted in making love much more frequently and with much more passion than the questions, "Hey, wanna have sex?" or, "You awake?" Their healing and growth in this area only came about because they were honest about their desires, and both took responsibility for co-creating a mutually satisfying intimacy.

When our children were young, our code question was, "Hey babe, is there any way we can get the children into bed early tonight?" But be forewarned, when that is your mission, your children will be of no help. Our daughters came equipped with an early warning intimacy detection system. The slightest touch of affection between the two of us would wake them from a deep sleep. Even now that they are adults, sometimes one of our phones will ring and we ask ourselves, "How did she know?"

What does not create intimacy, but for a husband may end with an obligatory orgasm, is his invocation of 1 Corinthians 7:3, "The husband should fulfill his marital duty to his wife, and likewise the wife to her husband." This verse leaves out the responsibilities that a husband has for co-creating a mutually satisfying intimacy.

For an authoritarian husband who feels the need to invoke this verse with his wife, who otherwise has no issues with sexual intimacy, our questions are, "What is missing from your relationship that causes her to not have that type of desire for you?" And, "How can that desire be rekindled?"

The irony for many couples is that they had "great sex" before marriage and almost none after. The passion of premarital sex was a substitute for building a mentally, emotionally, spiritually, and physically healthy relationship. Marriage is a single step on a lifelong journey to wholeness and relationship oneness. It begins best by building a conscious relationship before getting married that is continued by building a conscious marriage after.

Acceptance and personal value

When you were dating you both felt accepted and valued by each other, which made you feel even better about yourselves; at least that is what Jack wrote about himself. Riding that rollercoaster of acceptance seems fine when it is going up emotionally and you feel valued, but when that acceptance is temporarily or permanently removed, you have no choice but to ride it down emotionally and feel worthless.

You can only see your true value when you see yourself through God's eyes, which is revealed by the fact that Jesus died for you, and the Holy Spirit chooses to live in and work through you. It is fine for you and Jack to feel emotionally fulfilled when you are connected; though neither of you should link your feelings of personal value and self-acceptance to being accepted by the other. No one should have that power over anyone. The saying, "Beauty is in the eye of the beholder" is fine as long as that eye is God's.

Caroline, one last caution about foot rubs with hand lotion that Beth learned the hard way. When Jack is finished, put on your slippers before trying to walk on a vinyl floor. ☺

In Him,

Rick

Subject: First Met, Connection, Responsibilities, and Intimacy

Rick and Georgeann, we are writing this together.

Our strategy is to go through your last two emails and address each topic in order. We'll try our best to use the headings you did to help you keep track. Sorry if we jump around a bit.

This is Caroline.

Decision-making

When we can't agree we do not use your "...praying, listening, and talking ..." approach. What we often do, (only when we can't agree so it isn't all the time), is Jack keeps talking and persuading until I get tired and give in. I will often say, "Just go ahead and do what you want." Unfortunately, that isn't good enough. He wants me to agree, even when I don't. I am happy to agree if I think he is right, but I feel like I am betraying myself if I act like I agree when I don't. How can we do this differently?

This is Jack.

Caroline is accurate in what she says. I have a better analytical mind than she does, so if she wants to tell me I am wrong, she needs to convince me. I'm not saying she isn't intelligent, or that she isn't a great mother. She sometimes knows things about people and how they are feeling before they themselves even know what it is. If you ever want someone to pray and go before the Lord for you, Caroline is the one. She often comes back with amazing insight though she never takes credit for it. She says it is the Holy Spirit who gives her the insight. I, on the other hand, can give you Chapter and Verse for just about anything. Unfortunately, sometimes in my quest to get my way I lose my way. This is one of those areas in which we are opposites, and from what we have learned from previous emails is why we were attracted to each other.

We will work more on giving each other grace and mercy. I think the reason we don't is there is this underlying unrest between us that flares up in various skirmishes. The sad thing is that now we are writing about it, it seems so petty...and it is. We need to also focus on what is going right, not only on what is going wrong.

Imago

We both aren't sure about this Imago thing. It sounds a bit hocus pocus; like we are just automated pawns in the selection process. When Caroline was growing up, her father was a hard charging executive who abused alcohol at night. When he was drunk, everyone was on edge. The kids and her mother would do anything not to set him off. I am definitely not an alcoholic.

I got drunk once in high school when we won State in wrestling and almost fell out of a moving car when I opened the passenger door. I would have if my buddy hadn't caught me by my belt with his right hand, which was no small feat since he was also steering the car with his left. I haven't had a drink since.

Caroline is nothing like my mother. My dad was always on the road for work and sometimes we wouldn't see him for weeks at a time. That left my mother with three young boys to keep disciplined, which she did quite sternly. She also had a career as a publicist, so my grandmother (Gammy) watched us after school and several evenings during the week. Gammy was amazing. When we came home from school she was always happy to see us. This time my use of the word *always* is accurate.

Romance phase

As opposed to the Imago, your thoughts on the romance phase make total sense to us. All of the passion and energy and anticipation was our drug of choice. You might call it a psychosis, but most psychotics don't seem as happy as we were. And now it appears we are stuck between the power struggle and the conscious marriage you described. We don't want to be in the power struggle. How do we deal with this?

This is Caroline.

Acceptance and competence

I will address your interest in learning more about Jack's need for acceptance and competence because he always makes excuses for his mom and dad when this topic comes up. Jack, once I write this you can erase anything that isn't true.

Jack and I started dating our sophomore year in high school and I have never heard his mother or father compliment him without following it with a criticism. It makes me so frustrated.

During Jack's senior year in baseball he pitched a no hitter shutout. They won two to nothing. The team went crazy. I was sitting with his parents and when Jack finally came up to see us he was beaming. His smile was from ear to ear. The first thing his dad said and I kid you not, "Good job. If you hadn't walked their best hitter twice you would have had a perfect game." His mom said, "Well yes, that would have been nice, but you did win." For an instant I saw sadness flood Jack's face. He looked down and said, "Yep." He quickly looked at me and said, "The team is going out to celebrate. I'll call you later." How could his dad say such a thing? And why didn't his mom call his dad out on it?

No matter what Jack did, it wasn't good enough. That night I found out from Jack that the coach had told him not to throw anything their best hitter could hit. Of course Jack would end up walking him twice! Even at that, on the guy's third at bat he swung at a ball that was way outside and ended up hitting a line drive that would have taken Jack's head off if he hadn't got his glove up in time. And guess who went two for three at bat, and hit a home run with a man on base…Jack!

My dad played high school sports with Jack's dad and he said Jack's dad was mediocre at best. A hard worker yes, but not very good.

Whenever Jack receives a compliment for anything, he always downplays it or explains how he could have done better. Even now when we are back home and people talk about that game he usually adds, "Yeah, but that wasn't a very good team."

This is Jack.

Caroline's description is accurate, but I always knew my parents loved me. The truth is that I had it a lot easier than my dad did from his dad. Grandpa was an absolute tyrant. Nobody escaped his criticisms. He's been dead for many years, but if he could be around when Jesus returns, he would no doubt tell Jesus to go back and try it again with numerous suggestions on how everything could have been done better.

Inner-child

As to this inner-child and anger thing, we aren't sure we buy it. If there's a child inside who is different from us, then who is in control and when? And, the idea of having pain that you can't feel is also unclear. Isn't it only pain when you can feel it?

This is Caroline.

Connection and friends

I suppose I am as you put it, Connector in Chief. To be honest, Jack doesn't have much opportunity to initiate because I always beat him to it, except when I am mad or hurt.

Leaving my girlfriends was definitely the kind of pain that I felt, and am still feeling. I didn't realize what we had with one another. To be known and accepted means so much to me. When we all saw one another during our last furlough we picked up right where we left off. It was like we had never been gone, yet it had been 10 months. I don't expect Jack to replace them, but being closer to him would make it easier.

We're moving on to your second email.

Nice idea for dinner and a stroll. Around here the dinner works, but the snakes are a bit too aggressive and poisonous for an evening stroll.

Areas of responsibility

We are pretty content with how we handle our responsibilities now that Jack is helping more. In the past when he would try to help he would just start doing things without asking me what I needed. We figured it out several months ago when I was frustrated making supper and he claimed he was helping me by picking up and putting away the kid's toys. That wasn't what I needed at the time. Now he straight out asks me what I need, and if I say "Nothing," he doesn't have the slightest guilt when he wanders off to do whatever he wants. Even so, I can tell he stays within earshot if I do need something.

Only, never, and always

Your warning about not being distracted by the words *only*, *never*, and *always* during an argument caused us to be a bit embarrassed because we both fall into that trap. You know, the long one word question when someone makes an accusatory statement containing the word always. The drug out response is, "A...l...w...a...y...s?!" We promised each other to do better.

Physical intimacy

As far as physical intimacy is concerned, I am very very fortunate. I have it much better than most of my girlfriends. Yes, girlfriends talk. Jack is a very patient and generous lover. He's blushing right now. ☺☺ I am serious though. He never forces himself on me. His saying is, "Be nice so you get invited back."

Acceptance and personal value

One benefit of these emails is that we notice each other more. We also think about our thoughts and feelings, and try not to just go through the motions of life. I know you wrote "We can only see our value when we see ourselves through God's eyes," but that isn't good enough for me. I want Jack to *see me* valuing him through my loving eyes. And I want to *see him* valuing me through his loving eyes. If this makes us vulnerable, then that's a risk we are willing to take.

Experiencing a godly marriage

In my first email I wrote about feeling alone when Jack told me I could not have him and he walked out of the room. You later asked me, "Where was Jesus? You were right. There are experiences I can never have as a godly wife if Jack isn't willing to be a godly husband to whom I can respond. It's the same for him. He can only experience his fullness when I am acting and responding as I should. If he wasn't willing to work with me to have the best marriage possible, I would be doomed to experience only what he desired and was willing to work for.

It's so unfair that the spouse who is least willing to be godly and work at building a mutually satisfying marriage has the power to cripple the experience of the other. Just as with acceptance and personal value, no one should have that power over someone else, though that is the way God has allowed to be.

We are both committed to becoming who God intended us to be and to build the marriage He wants us to have. And it's not just for our children; it's for us as well. We do not have to continue suffering. We can change.

We will close for now because we want to get to bed early. Thanks for the warning about vinyl floors. ☺ As athletic as Beth is, that would have been hilarious to see.

Best always,

Caroline and Jack

Subject: Re: First Met, Connection, Responsibilities, and Intimacy

Jack and Caroline, this is Rick.

Discernment

Caroline, it sounds like you have discernment, which can be a very difficult gift. The main problem is that you sense or know something before others do, and if you share it, some people who do not understand the gift want to know your logic. It's DISCERNMENT; not logic. ☺

When I was practicing as an employed veterinarian in Virginia Beach, Georgeann tried to warn me about a woman who was flirting with me. I told Georgeann that she was being too sensitive and it was just friendly banter. Later it became obvious that the woman had intentions other than friendly banter. I came home and told Georgeann that I would never disregard her discernment again.

Georgeann's discernment is so important to me that if I have a business deal that I am considering, I insist that both of us have dinner with the other person and his or her spouse if married. I want Georgeann to sniff them to make sure they're okay. Georgeann prefers the word "scan" to "sniff." I also watch how the other couple interacts with each other. I have found that people who treat their spouse with respect usually treat their business partners with the same. In addition, that spouse can become the unofficial and not so silent partner in the business.

Jack, an analytical mind is a wonderful thing, but some very important forces cannot be analyzed using logic.

Grace and mercy

Caroline, I'm glad you and Jack are giving each other more grace and mercy. A friend of mine once explained the difference. Grace is giving someone something good they do not deserve, and mercy is withholding something bad that they do deserve. We strive to give both to each other when needed.

Imago

The Imago that we wrote about is not a fixed set of easily discerned characteristics, and is much more complex than anyone can fully comprehend. We just look for patterns, tendencies, and subtle similarities among past and current relationships. For example, Caroline, from what we have learned about you, you sound a lot like Jack's grandmother. You are warm, nurturing, and engaging with your children, and you are the same with Jack when the two of you are getting along. I know it sounds weird that Jack was attracted to someone like his grandmother when he got to know you, but it makes sense that Jack's ideal image of a nurturer would be patterned partially by his experiences with her. He was subconsciously and consciously looking for someone who matched the impression she left on him.

Jack, in the same way for Caroline, it is true that you are not an alcoholic, but from one of her emails, it does seem like you have high standards for achievement that are difficult for others, including yourself, to attain. In the same way, alcoholics often have standards for others that are difficult to live up to such as, read my mind, anticipate and provide for what I want when I want it, and stay out of my way.

Alcoholics, like people who claim to be perfectionists, can also be unpredictable as to what sets them off. Once you think you understand their rules, they change them. This means that as a child you can do one thing one day and they proclaim how cute you are, and you do the same thing the next and they criticize you for being stupid. This type of inconsistency is disruptive to a child's mental and emotional safety as he or she tries to identify the family rules and behaviors for acceptance and belonging.

Defenses and survival strategies

Jack, as I just wrote, Caroline grew up around a high achieving and hard charging father who at times was unpredictable. Perhaps that is initially what made her feel comfortable with you because your characteristics were familiar to her. I am not criticizing you or her father. I have no idea what his inner pressures were, or what his desires, needs, fears, wounds, defenses, and assumptions may have been. He may have been doing life as well as he could. The problem is that if you trigger Caroline's defenses and emotional reactions from that period of her life, she will react to you as though you were him. And, she will probably react with the same emotions she had at that age. That is why in retrospect, what is said during many arguments seems childish.

If Caroline's survival strategy was to withdraw and become invisible, there's a good chance she will do that with you. Conversely, if her survival strategy was to fight back, she will likely do the same with you. Then again, those children who were withdrawn and passive when young often respond by becoming aggressive and attacking when adults.

Parents pass on what they have

The vast majority of parents do the best they can for their children using whatever mental and emotional resources they have. They often pass on the rules and behaviors that helped them either thrive or survive in childhood and adulthood. Unfortunately, if they grew up in a stressed and dysfunctional family system, when they are adults their own family may become trapped in the same cycle. The rules and behaviors that made sense to them growing up, may do little more than pass on the same pain to their children. It is very difficult for parents to give their children what they as children never had or saw in others. That is why anyone who wants to break the cycle of a destructive family system, must look to new role models with healthy rules and behaviors.

Power struggle and conscious marriage

The power struggle and conscious marriage are not discrete categories that the two of you once and for all pass from one to the other. A marriage is a shifting and ongoing blend of both. It is the amount of time the two of you spend in one or the other that is a measure of your growth together. Actually, you *spend* time in the power struggle and *invest* time in a conscious marriage.

Couples who succeed in living more and more in a conscious marriage learn that getting what they want when they want it, or close to what they want when they want it, is more likely to occur when both are cooperating with each other, as opposed to one trying to exert power over the other. The power approach may get someone what they want, but it always diminishes their spouse, which over time takes a toll on their relationship. Of course, abusers do not care if or how they diminish their spouse as long as they get what they want when they want it. Their emotional state is that of a demanding small child. To be honest, demanding small children are often more reasonable.

Perfectionism

Jack, Caroline's description of your father and mother sheds light on your issues of perfection, and feeling attacked and incompetent when she criticizes you. It can be a replay of countless experiences growing up. Your strong feelings can indicate that you are still carrying the childhood wound of having to be perfect to win their acceptance and approval. Many people who carry this wound think of God and see Him as having the same characteristics as their disapproving parent. This idea is best expressed In the Heart of Man, when William Paul Young, author of The Shack, said "It took me all of fifty years to wipe the face of my father completely off the face of God." The opposite is also true. An earthly father who is loving, merciful, and gives grace, lays the foundation for his children to better understand God and His love, mercy, and grace.

Perfectionism is a game you can never win; there is no perfection in relationships or anything else. For people who play the perfectionism game, self-criticism is rarely silenced, and they must endure a continuous running dialog of accusations. I'm not saying that we should never criticize ourselves because we should if we have done something poorly. For example, if you are confronted by someone at church and you let your emotions get the best of you, you would do well to figure out how and why it happened so you could prevent it from happening again.

On the other hand, let's go back to your no hitter shutout and how you might have tormented yourself if perfection was your goal. Even if no one got on base, you could criticize yourself for how many times batters made contact with the ball. And if you struck out every batter, you could criticize yourself for how many balls you threw compared to strikes. And if you only threw sixty-three pitches over seven innings, you could criticize yourself that each pitch did not arrive perfectly where you meant to throw it.

Self-criticism and identity

People who are intent on criticizing themselves do not stop until they find failure, no matter how small, trivial, or nonexistent. The problem often is that even though they want to be accepted, they feel uncomfortable when they are, and will do their best to beat themselves back to the familiar feelings of failure. They often do this because success is not consistent with their core identity. Their logic, conscious or not, often is, "My identity in the family is that I am a failure. If I want to be accepted in this family I need to play the failure role that I have been assigned. Therefore, I am a failure, and when it looks like I might be successful, I sabotage myself." Or, another common thought is, "If I am successful, people will expect more of me, and I don't want to work hard enough to live up to my potential and their expectations."

Some people think their success is the result of being harsh with themselves. In reality, they were likely to be successful despite how much they beat themselves up in the process. There is no telling how successful they would have been if in addition to their high standards and hard work, they also were kind and encouraging to themselves.

One last thought: Our own self-criticism influences how we think God views us. Just as Paul Young had to wipe the face of his father off of God's face, sometimes we need to wipe our own face off of God's face.

It's getting late. I'll write more tomorrow about the concepts of intent, inner-child, wounds, and defenses.

Good night,

Rick

Subject: Intent, Inner-Child, Wounds, and Defenses

Jack and Caroline, this is Rick.

Intent

Jack, I noticed your response to Caroline's description of your dad and mother was that she was accurate, and you added that you, "always knew your parents loved you." Intent is important, but does not justify everything a parent does. Some parents punish their children harshly so they won't grow up to be defiant. Some parents constantly criticize their teenager's appearance in order to motivate him or her to always look attractive so as not to be rejected by others. The tragedy is that these parenting behaviors can leave a child feeling broken and not accepted by their parent.

We've often had people try to minimize or justify their childhood wounds from parents and others. The first question we ask is, "Does that mean it is okay for you or someone else to treat your child the same way you were treated?" Usually the person gives us a steely-eyed look and says something to the effect of "Never!" That's when they see how they really feel.

Inner-child

When we think of an inner-child, it isn't in the context of one personality or another in the same way that people can have multiple personalities. It is more like having multiple facets on a diamond or multiple channels on a TV. For example, someone can be one way at work, another at home, and another at church with all three being appropriate for their environment. Some facets can be more playful and less guarded than others. I have a friend who is a police officer. He really is a big teddy bear. That said, he has a game face and body stance that when it is needed projects pure power. Bad guys in the street don't like it and he doesn't abuse it. In the same way we can have emotional game faces.

Emotional triggers

Caroline, when Jack was criticized by his dad he had to hide his anger because his dad and mother would have no capacity to help him process it. As a result, his anger was stored. When you criticize him, or when he perceives that what you say is criticism, it can trigger him to revert back emotionally to that time in his life, which then releases the anger that he felt and could not express at that time. This is where triggers have great value.

It is in recognizing triggers and exploring their emotional forces that wounds are discovered and healing can occur. People often ask, "How do I know it was a trigger?" It's a trigger when your emotional response is far greater than what the offense warranted. Causes include a buildup of daily stresses, recent events, long-term stresses, past wounds, or a combination of the four and others. The next time you are arguing, ask yourselves, How old do I feel emotionally? When have I felt this way before? What is the youngest age I remember feeling this way?

One last thought about anger. Anger that is stored can be expressed as self-loathing and depression. It can also be expressed throughout the body by an almost unlimited number of symptoms. That is why accepting and processing anger is so important for mental, emotional, spiritual, and physical health.

Wounds and defenses

Identifying wounds, understanding their cause, and removing the defenses around them is critical for healing and growth. Reactive and relationship-destructive defenses must be replaced with intentional and healthy responses. This doesn't mean that defenses are permanently discarded because there may be situations where they are appropriate.

For example, think of a man who is prone to getting into and finishing fights. Now picture his or someone else's family being attacked. In that situation his ability to fight is essential for their survival, and makes him a righteous warrior. The problem, however, is when the appropriate godly response in a confrontation is to turn the other cheek, but he insists on fighting. Our defenses are fine if they do not get in the way of God's will for us and something we want more, such as connection with our spouse, children, and friends.

Caroline, this is Georgeann.

Connection and friends

I have left friends in exactly the same way you described. It was crushing. My heart goes out to you and your friends. All I can suggest is that you continue to pray for one another and be intentional about calling and writing when you can, and if at all possible, make time to be together whenever you are in the States.

When it comes to friends, Jack can be a great husband, but he cannot take the place of your friends. That said, Jack should ideally be closer and more trustworthy than your best friend. What I mean is that Rick and I are spouses and we are closer to each other than we are to any of our friends. That doesn't mean we don't have several wonderful friends, it just means they are not as close to us as we are to each other.

Unfortunately, we have known people who use their best friend as a substitute for their spouse. This indicates a void in their struggling marriage. When this is the case, the solution is to work towards healing and growth in their marriage, while maintaining a close relationship with their friend.

Definitely sorry to hear about the snakes! I don't like snakes and am very suspicious of spiders. Many years ago I was barefoot in the garage and stepped on a large corn spider. Whenever I think about it I can still feel the prickly hairs in the arch of my foot. ☹

Take care,

Georgeann

Subject: Re: Re: First Met, Connection, Responsibilities, and Intimacy

Rick and Georgeann, this is Caroline.

Discernment

The problem with my discernment is that I don't know if it is always true in the same way I really know something. I know the recipe for Jack's favorite dish. If someone challenges me on it I can whip out the envelope that his grandmother wrote it on. With my discernment, I think I am sure, but not 100%. God doesn't give me that kind of absolute clarity and certainty.

When I tell someone something that I think is from God, I will often ask if it makes sense to them. Most of the time they say yes, but sometimes they say no. Occasionally, I have had a bad feeling of discernment about a person that didn't make sense, only to find out later that what I was sensing was true. I know 1 Corinthians 23:7 says that love "always protects, always trusts, always hopes, always perseveres," but I believe I can still love people with God's love even if I do not trust them. That is when I have to trust God that He is in control and will reveal what needs to be revealed at the right time.

I've heard that explanation of grace and mercy before, though it's always good to be reminded.

Being compared favorably to Jack's grandmother is quite the compliment. She was an absolutely lovely woman. How she got matched up with Jack's grandfather is still a mystery to me. She was a very kind, gentle, and funny lady. One time she said to me that divorce had never crossed her mind, though thoughts of murder had.

This is Jack.

Wounds and defenses

Well crap! This idea in your last email that wounds and defenses are just replicated in each generation is pretty depressing. You are saying that my defensive reaction of anger towards my father is triggered when Caroline criticizes me! And, her defensive reaction of withdrawing from her father is triggered when I point out something I think could have been done better. When do we get to live our lives apart from what we went through growing up? It's like we are reenacting a civil war battle using live ammunition! The worst part is that if we don't change these patterns, we are going to roll this ball of pain right onto our children, which they will roll onto theirs. How do we make this vicious cycle stop?

Caroline and I still spend plenty of time in the power struggle, which we do not enjoy. It seems that in a conscious marriage we would have power *with* each other, not *over* each other.

My experience in wrestling is of no help because that was all about power and exerting my will. When an opponent walked onto MY mat, I made sure he didn't want to do it again.

Based on what both of you are telling us it is clear we have many childhood wounds and defenses. Believe it or not, I do pray over these emails and ask God to show me my heart along with my wounds and defenses.

Perfectionism

I had some interesting insight on this perfectionist thing. Here is the logic. A pianist can play the piano. A gymnast can do gymnastics. A perfectionist cannot do perfection. So, no one can call themselves a perfectionist because a perfectionist needs to do perfect. Even people who call themselves a perfectionist will agree that no one, including themselves, is perfect. When I shared this with Caroline her response was, "You really just want things a specific way." That's when I realized that I am not a perfectionist, I'm a specifist! At first I felt bad about not realizing this before, but even my spellchecker had not heard of it. My real problem is specifism, not perfectionism.

As far as your concern about me being critical and harsh with myself, I think I should start charging you rent for living in my head! The good news is there's no issue with me self-sabotaging or being lazy.

In wrestling, nothing short of a pin was good enough, and if the other guy scored points prior to the pin, it didn't feel like a real win. The next worst was if I only won on points...to me it was a loss. I don't even want to think about the matches I lost because the following week my wrestling partner paid a steep price for them. You also "pinned" my dad so to speak because even if I pinned my opponent his question would be, "How could you have pinned him sooner?" I remember my senior year when wrestling was over, deep inside I was glad. Given what it took out of me, I'm not sure I could have kept going for another year.

Intent

As to my parent's intent when I was growing up, intent is everything. I realize that good intent can still leave wounds, but bad intent is just unthinkable. Sometimes good intent is all I have left to cling to when I think about my parenting of Billy and Erica. Your question about how I would react if "other people" treated one of my children the way my dad treated me was interesting. If they did, I would probably end up doing some jail time.

This is Caroline.

Stored emotions

We are starting to get this idea that wounds and the emotions that come with them can be stored if they are not dealt with at the time of the wounding. They certainly don't get better with age. It's just hard to know when we are dealing with an old wound, or a real and present aggravation.

Loved your questions for when we are arguing. How old do I feel emotionally? When have I felt this way before? What is the youngest age I remember feeling this way? We didn't have to wait for another argument to apply them; we have plenty to look back on.

Talking through an argument

Last night we talked through an argument we had several months ago when I was trying to fix a broken picture frame. Jack reached in and took it from my hands to help, which did not make me happy at all. I yelled at him and told him if I wanted his help I would ask for it! Jack reacted and came back at me with how he was just trying to help and I should be grateful that he was the kind of husband who wanted to. So with that argument in mind, we went through your questions.

I felt like I was in junior high school when my dad butted in and took over a science project I was working on. When Jack reached in and took the picture frame, a switch flipped in my head and I felt like that same junior high school girl who was angry at her father. This time, however, the anger was free-flowing. It made perfect sense based on what I was saying to Jack and how I was saying it. Jack told me that at the time he thought I was acting very childish over something as insignificant as a picture frame. As we now realize, I was acting exactly how I should expect, given I felt like I was in junior high school again. It took Jack a while to realize that he had his own childhood reactions towards me during the argument.

We also talked about how frustrated I was with my dad when I was growing up. I didn't know how to set and defend a boundary between his desire to help and my need to become more independent. We talked about how much I loved my dad, and why this trait of his was so irritating. Dad did this all of the time with the family; taking over what they were trying to do. With Beth, however, it was a different story. With her, if he tried he would have pulled back a bloody stump. She was fierce about her projects and what she worked on, and as you know, still is.

The more Jack and I talked, it became clear that I still have the same insecurities I had as a child about being able to do things on my own. Anyone who tries to help without my request only reinforces my deeply held belief that I am incompetent. How ironic is it that Jack and I both struggle with feelings of incompetence? His defense is to try harder and harder, and mine is to pull back and play it safe. We should take notes and learn from each other's healing.

Even though it was really difficult that evening to plow through such painful stuff, it was great because we did it together. I cried and so did Jack. I was able to forgive and let go of my dad's intrusion once I realized what it was, and how it was still festering in me. That's the only way I could be free of it.

We even realized why when Jack intrudes on something Erica is doing, I boldly step in and tell him to let her figure it out on her own. I have no trouble recognizing and defending Erica from his uninvited intrusions, but find it difficult to stand up for myself in a firm and respectful way. Until now, I had never linked my conviction to defend Erica's independence with my dad's intrusions. I just always felt compelled to do so.

I also told Jack that the picture frame argument wasn't his fault, my fault, or even our fault, because neither of us knew what was driving our emotions and reactions.

At the time, he felt rejected because I didn't want to receive his help. What made it so painful for him is that helping others is at the core of his being. He's always trying to rescue or save someone. During our training for the mission field, a pastor told him that he had a "Savior Complex," and unless he let go of it, someday it would cause him to resent others and burn out.

Connection and friends

Georgeann, Jack and I are closer to each other than we are to any of our friends, but sometimes I need to talk something through with someone other than Jack; especially if it's about him. I only do this, however, with wise women who are not prone to inflame the situation. Unfortunately, we've known women and men who were so unhappy in their own relationship that they tried to tear down the relationships of others. You have to be really careful who you go to for advice.

Time to start supper. Jack has been at the church. I'll let him read through this before I send it. Hope this "efficient" strategy works better for us this time than it did the last. ☺

This is Jack.

Specifist and an irrational perfectionist

While I was walking to church I realized that I am a specifist and an irrational perfectionist! I want others to do things the specific way I want, and I expect perfection from myself. This is totally irrational. The more emails we exchange the worse I'm getting. ☺

The more I think about it, specifism isn't bad with something like brain surgery, as opposed to the best way to sweep the floor, fold the laundry, or load the dishwasher; speaking of which, we truly miss having one.

Caroline just told me there is in fact a specific way the dishwasher should be loaded. Is that true? She said she would teach me when we get back to the States. Oh well, batting two for three on my examples isn't bad. I don't have to be perfect. See, I'm getting better already! ☺

Blessings,

Jack

Subject: Discernment, Active Listening, and Breaking Old Patterns

Caroline, this is Georgeann.

Discernment

Sometimes when people do not think what you are telling them is from God, and it is accurate, it may mean that God has not yet revealed to them everything they need to know. What you told them may be what was needed to get them thinking and seeking God. The bottom line is you need to step out in faith and trust God to do the rest. By the way, if someone vehemently disagrees with what you are telling them, it may be accurate and something that God has already been speaking to them about, but they have been unwilling to listen to Him. Give them time and don't lose faith in your gift. Of course, there is always the possibility you could be wrong. We are not perfect followers of Jesus, and it takes time and practice for us to become competent in our gifting.

One time Rick was given a strong and condemning word from a close friend. Rick prayed about it and talked with me, and we did not see any application in his life. As circumstances unfolded, we realized that the word was absolutely true regarding something in his friend's life, and had nothing to do with Rick at all. In essence, his friend received the right message from God, but delivered it to the wrong address.

Jack and Caroline, this is Rick.

Breaking the cycle of triggers and defenses

The first step in breaking the "vicious cycle" of triggers that cause childhood defenses to spring into action is to first recognize them and choose to respond differently. In the beginning, this recognition usually occurs a few days after an argument. Later, you and Caroline will begin to recognize these patterns sooner. Eventually you will catch yourselves falling into these old patterns in the middle of an argument and hopefully someone calls, "Timeout!" At that point the two of you have a choice. You either choose to continue the same cycle of wounding and re-wounding from the past, or you seize the courage that God offers in that moment to try and turn away from the power struggle, embrace a conscious marriage, and build something different.

Speaking-listening-mirroring-clarifying

When you catch yourselves in an unfruitful pattern, either or both of you need to take a break to cool off. Once the two of you get back together, you agree that someone will be the speaker and the other will listen.

The speaker shares small segments of his or her position and the listener mirrors back by repeating what was heard. Then the listener asks, "Did I repeat that back correctly?" The speaker verifies that the mirroring was correct, and if not, provides clarification. After each segment of speaking-listening-mirroring-clarifying, the listener responds with, "Is there more to that?" This cycle is repeated until the person who is speaking believes that the listener understands his or her position.

For mirroring to be effective, it is absolutely essential that the listener is genuinely curious about the speaker's position, and then validates that person's thoughts and feelings.

There is always the temptation for the listener to interrupt in order to defend his or her position. This is never helpful and almost always restarts the power struggle.

It is important to note that validating someone's thoughts and feelings does not mean you agree with them. It only means that you understand how and why they think and feel what they do.

It is also important for the listener to be patient because many times the person doing the talking does not fully understand what he or she thinks and feels until it is spoken. When the first person doing the speaking feels understood, then you switch roles and repeat the process.

Eventually, you will internalize the spirit of this mirroring process and it will become a natural part of your thinking and dialogue. This means you won't always have to adhere to the rigid structure. Even so, you may need to come back to it if passions are high and listening is low. One guy told me this sounded like it would take a lot of time. I asked him, "How long does it usually take for you and your wife to argue, stay mad, and get communication back to normal?" He said, "Days." I assured him this process would not take that long. ☺

Wrestling and renewing your mind

You mentioned that your wrestling experience was of no help, which is only partially true. It's true that wrestling with Caroline mentally and emotionally isn't helpful, but wrestling with your own thoughts and emotions to bring every thought captive to Christ is. In 2 Corinthians 10:5 the Apostle Paul wrote, "We demolish arguments and every pretension that sets itself up against the knowledge of God, and we take captive every thought to make it obedient to Christ." Taking thoughts captive begins with Romans 12: 1-2,

> Therefore, I urge you, brothers and sisters, in view of God's mercy, to offer your bodies as a living sacrifice, holy and pleasing to God — this is your true and proper worship. 2 Do not conform to the pattern of this world, but be transformed by the renewing of your mind. Then you will be able to test and approve what God's will is — his good, pleasing and perfect will.

Next comes Philippians 4:8 where Paul talks about what thoughts to foster. "Finally, brothers and sisters, whatever is true, whatever is noble, whatever is right, whatever is pure, whatever is lovely, whatever is admirable — if anything is excellent or praiseworthy — think about such things."

So Jack, the progression from conflict to peaceful resolution is for you to bring every thought captive by first offering yourself to God as a living sacrifice, and then with Caroline in mind, think about what is true, noble, right, pure, lovely, admirable, excellent, or praiseworthy about her. Caroline, you do the same with Jack. With this as a foundation, the two of you can effectively engage, listen, and speak the truth in love.

Engaging becomes easier when both of you establish new rules and behaviors for interacting, and you experience the joy of safe and effective communication. It is in this safety that your true thoughts and feelings can be expressed and understood. The result is your individual healing and growth that leads to a mutually satisfying marriage.

Unfortunately, what often happens is that couples revert back to their childhood emotions and lash out at each other to defend themselves, prevent the re-wounding of old wounds, or to simply get what they want. The opposite usually occurs in that old wounds are re-wounded, new wounds are added, what is wanted is rarely received, and unproductive defenses are reinforced.

This type of fighting back is often needed to survive a chaotic and destructive family, or for pinning someone on a wrestling mat. But, for a marriage relationship, it only multiplies and intensifies the pain. And, if fighting back remains the norm, it eventually results in the death of the relationship and possibly divorce. We have seen far too many marriages that were relationally dead with both people only going through the motions. That said, all relationships can be brought back from the dead if both people are willing to do the work and have the tools, insight, and energy to do so. Wanting a great marriage is essential, but not sufficient. Couples must do the hard work that is needed to build one, especially when they don't want to.

Awareness and stopping the cycle

Jack, I know it is painful for you to agree with Caroline's observation that you are starting to parent Billy in the same way your dad parented you, and how your grandfather parented him. What is encouraging is that now you know and want to stop. Awareness of what was passed down is the first step in either stopping it or, at the least, slowing it down considerably. It is like a hot potato being passed from one generation to another, and you decide to hold onto it until it either cools or burns through your hands.

I have often heard parents say they would do anything for their children, even die for them. Sometimes the most important and meaningful act that parents can do is to work through their own painful past in order to build a better future for themselves, their spouse, and their children. Not that all of one's past is painful, but it's the painful parts that often drive our negative thoughts and emotions, which can strongly determine how we relate to our family and others.

Caroline, this is Georgeann.

What a great idea to use the picture frame argument from the past to learn how to manage triggers and defenses! That's much easier than trying to do so in real-time during an argument.

I will summarize what you described so you will fully appreciate what you and Jack accomplished. Jack's behavior triggered your reaction that was based on a past wound. By talking about the trigger and linking it to the past, you were able to surface the past wound and be intentional about forgiving your father. You and Jack were also able to understand what happened in order to avoid the same trigger in the future. You experienced healing and growth for the past and you also strengthen your marriage in the present. That was perfect. Yes, Jack, it was perfect! ☺

Jack, this is Rick again.

That was great insight about you being both a *specifist* with others, and an *irrational perfectionist* with yourself. I wish I had thought of it.

I have been instructed on the proper loading of a dishwasher and it makes total sense...to do it the way Georgeann or Caroline wants. ☺

Keep praying, loving, and applying what you are learning.

In Him,

Rick and Georgeann

Subject: Betrayal

Rick and Georgeann, this is Caroline.

Wow, Georgeann! I can't believe how well you and Rick handled his friend's betrayal with the condemning word that was from God, but not for Rick. How could you ever trust that person again?

When Rick wrote to us about stopping the "vicious cycle" of triggers and defensive reactions by first recognizing when it happens AFTER the conflict, Jack's response was, "I guess improvement begins by failing for shorter and shorter periods of time."☺ As strange as that sounds, I think Jack is right. We would still suffer the pain from an argument for not handling it well, but at least we wouldn't suffer as long before we worked it out.

Rick, this is Jack.

2 Corinthians 10:5 is impossible. No one I know can do the "…we take captive every thought to make it obedient to Christ" thing. I mean I just get frustrated being told to do things in Scripture that are not possible. Ephesians 5:25 is a perfect example. "Husbands, love your wives, just as Christ loved the church and gave himself up for her." Do you love Georgeann as "Christ loved the church?" Do you give yourself up for her in the way He did for His church? If you do, you are light-years ahead of me and anything I will ever be.

What about verse 33 in the same chapter. Do you love Georgeann in the same way as you love yourself? And, if we go with your Pre-Fall model of marriage where a husband and wife are coequal, doesn't that mean Caroline should love ME as Christ loved the church, and she should love ME in the same way she loves herself? I'm not trying to be difficult. I'm just tired of Christian teaching that sets the bar so high I can't possibly get over it. Caroline can't get over it either.

On another topic, what you wrote about a marriage being "relationally dead and going through the motions" troubles me because Caroline and I both feel like sometimes we are just "going through the motions." Does that make our relationship dead? That is really discouraging.

Georgeann, thank you for outlining in detail how well we did processing our argument from the past. We thought we only talked about it until you explained everything that happened; the healing and such. We're so messed up we can't even appreciate it when we do something really well. Though to our credit, we have been trying to become better listeners to make sure we understand each other. The mirroring process still feels weird; not sure we'll ever get around to doing it exactly the way Rick described. No offense Rick.

Jack

Subject: Re: Betrayal

Caroline, this is Georgeann.

Betrayal and sincerity

As for Rick's friend and the misdirected word from God, it wasn't betrayal. Rick's friend was completely sincere and had been used mightily by God in many other situations. This particular one was too close to his own life for him to see, which can happen to any of us. Even though Rick's friend was sincere, sincerity is not enough because we have all been sincerely wrong at one time or another.

We should weigh carefully in our mind and spirit not only what we share with someone, but also what we are offered. This includes what we as spouses offer each other while we are working through our own healing and growth. If you think what someone offers you is incorrect it is perfectly fine to reply, "I do not receive that."

Betrayal is when people intentionally take advantage of your relationship to achieve their own gains, or have a total disregard for your relationship when pursuing their own agenda. Cheating on a spouse, using a threat to get what one wants, or embezzling from an employer are examples of betrayal.

Rick was asked by a one of his veterinary students, "Why is it that friends are the ones who stab you in the back?" He thought for a moment and replied, "Because they are the ones you let back there." This doesn't mean you shouldn't trust your friends, or your spouse, it just means you need to trust Jesus for your healing if things go poorly.

All relationships have risks and Matthew 10:16 is still relevant today. Jesus told His disciples, "I am sending you out like sheep among wolves. Therefore be as shrewd as snakes and as innocent as doves." Don't be surprised if you and Jack find wolves faithfully attending church.

Manipulation or motivation

This is a good time for me to share with you the difference between manipulation and motivation; especially in how it applies to marriage. Manipulation is getting someone to achieve *your* goal, of which, that person is unaware. Motivation, on the other hand, is helping someone achieve *their* goal, of which, they are aware and have asked you to help.

For example, now that Jack knows he wants to do a better job at parenting, he can invite you into helping him by giving you permission to identify what he is doing well and what he can improve upon. Both of you share the goal and he knows and approves of how you are trying to help.

An example of manipulation would be a husband who participated in the mirroring technique of communication that Rick described with the sole purpose of deceiving his wife into thinking he cared and was trustworthy. Sadly, we have seen couples where one or both spouses only wanted the appearance of working on their marriage and had no intention of changing anything except their spouse's behavior.

Motivation with insight in the power of the Holy Spirit is what Rick and I try to do to help people achieve their marriage goals, and understand and accept their individual roles for doing so. We try very hard not to impose our marriage goals and roles on them. Bob and Beth are perfect examples in that they are happily married, and both are growing more and more into their own unique image of Jesus. That said, their goals, and more specifically, the roles they maintain to achieve those goals would not fit well for me and Rick, or you and Jack. They struggled with this for quite awhile because they were so different from their friends and family. They didn't have any obvious role models to study.

Jack, this is Rick.

Sometimes you amaze me. Yes, failing for shorter and shorter periods of time is, in fact, being more and more successful.

Impossible-to-perform verses

I agree with you that "no one can take captive every thought to make it obedient to Christ," and that the Scriptures are full of impossible-to-perform verses. It is important to remember that these are not high bars to achieve, rather, they are the Holy Spirit's power to receive. We can't do any of this in our own strength. As the Apostle Paul writes in Philippians,

> Therefore, my dear friends, as you have always obeyed — not only in my presence, but now much more in my absence — continue to work out your salvation with fear and trembling, [13] for it is God who works in you to will and to act in order to fulfill his good purpose. (Philippians 2:12-13)

We work out our salvation with God who works in us to will and to act. Remember that Jesus fulfilled the Law as Paul writes in Romans Chapter 8.

> Therefore, there is now no condemnation for those who are in Christ Jesus, [2] because through Christ Jesus the law of the Spirit who gives life has set you free from the law of sin and death. [3] For what the law was powerless to do because it was weakened by the flesh, God did by sending his own Son in the likeness of sinful flesh to be a sin offering. And so he condemned sin in the flesh, [4] in order that the righteous requirement of the law might be fully met in us, who do not live according to the flesh but according to the Spirit. (Romans 8:1-4)

I intellectually understand this and it is still a constant struggle for me, or anyone else, to stay in the Spirit. (Here it comes again. ☺) We need an ongoing renewing of our mind as in Romans 12:1-2.

> Therefore, I urge you, brothers and sisters, in view of God's mercy, to offer your bodies as a living sacrifice, holy and pleasing to God — this is your true and proper worship. [2] Do not conform to the pattern of this world, but be transformed by the renewing of your mind. Then you will be able to test and approve what God's will is — his good, pleasing and perfect will.

We cannot do any of this Christian stuff on our own. Sure, sometimes we can *act* like Jesus, but He wants to *live in* us and *work through* us. That is why we are the temple of the Holy Spirit. The Apostle Paul wrote to the Corinthians about this.

> Do you not know that your bodies are temples of the Holy Spirit, who is in you, whom you have received from God? You are not your own; [20] you were bought at a price. Therefore honor God with your bodies. (1 Corinthians 6:19-20)

Anything spiritual we do begins with us offering ourselves as a living sacrifice and realizing that we are the temple of the Holy Spirit. Then God can produce His will in us and accomplish His purposes through us.

You asked if I love Georgeann as "Christ loved the church?" And, do I give myself up for her the way Jesus did for His church? Of course not. Am I getting better at it over the years? Absolutely. Would I have been able to get as far as I have on my own without God working in and through me? Absolutely not.

Going through the motions

As for you and Caroline "going through the motions," this isn't bad if it is godly obedience that overcomes temporary feelings of disconnection. Unfortunately, going through the motions can also serve the purpose of ungodly avoidance that solidifies permanent feelings of disconnection. Godly obedience maintains your relationship, while ungodly avoidance starves your relationship. Godly obedience is about function and substance, while ungodly avoidance is about function and appearance. Godly obedience supports your healing and growth, while ungodly avoidance maintains wounds and defenses.

And, as for the question of whether or not the relationship is dead, if spouses are asking the question, it isn't. I have heard it said that the opposite of love is indifference.

Jack and Caroline , this is Georgeann.

Unrecognized success

We've lost count of the number of times a couple has thought they messed up when they actually did great. Here's how the conversation usually unfolds.

So how did the week go?

> Not so well.

Really? What happened?

> We had an argument.

What about?

> <Fill in any number of topics here>

Tell us more.

> We were both tired, and about 20 minutes into the argument we decided to stop and get supper because the kids were hungry.

Then what happened?

> After supper we finished the dishes and got the kids bathed and in bed. Then he asked if I wanted to talk more about it. I said, "Not really. But I will if you want to." He thought we should. He said he wanted to understand what I was upset about and he was willing to listen.

> I told him I was frustrated all day, the kids were on a sugar-high from playing at the neighbor's, and I felt like he had been ignoring me. When I was finished, I asked him what he was so upset about. He said he had a whole list of stuff that had gone wrong at work and he just wanted a peaceful home as a refuge. As it turned out, most of what got us so upset with each other had nothing to do with us.

How did it end?

> What do you mean, "How did it end?"

I mean what did you do next?

We went to bed.

Did you go to bed okay with each other?

Well, yeah. We went to sleep.

I thought you said your week didn't go well.

It didn't. We had an argument.

No, you had a disagreement that became an argument. You stopped the argument when you realized you had other more pressing things to do. You got back together to talk it out. You explained yourselves to each other and both of you listened. Then you went to bed and you were okay with each other. Is that right?

Yeah.

Are you kidding me? You did everything just right. We all have disagreements that become arguments. Success is how quickly you reach an understanding.

Congratulations! You had a great week!

Really?! Guess we did.

Jack, this is Rick.

Garden of Eden mutual love

In your last email you wrote, "…your Pre-Fall model of marriage…" I don't think it is *my* model. ☺

What you asked about Caroline having the same responsibility for loving you as you do for loving her is exactly true. According to the Pre-Fall model of marriage, you and Caroline should have mutual love for each other. You are to love her as Christ loves the Church, and as you love yourself. And, she is to love you as Christ loves the Church, and as she loves herself. It is difficult to argue credibly that spouses should not be growing in their ability to have the same love for each other because they are both being conformed into the image of Jesus. Of course, this is the ideal, and the reality is that there will always be a difference between spouses in their ability and choice to love each other.

We cannot surprise God

You and Caroline ask great questions and come up with some really wise insight. I appreciate the honesty that both of you bring to our relationship. I also know that God appreciates your honesty as well. We may as well be honest with Him because He knows everything.

When we accept Jesus and His blood for our sins, God doesn't accept us the way we might accept a friend, only to be hurt later by his or her unanticipated failing or betrayal. When God accepts us, He already knows everything we have done and everything we will ever think, say, and do; our successes and our failures. On what basis in the future would He reject us? The only ones surprised in the future by what we think, say, and do is us.

In Him,

Rick and Georgeann

Subject: No Mentors to Follow

Rick and Georgeann, this is Jack.

We were up late last night talking. The subject line of this email pretty much covers it. We know you have been really successful with Beth and Bob, but just as you wrote in your last email, their marriage doesn't speak to us. Don't get us wrong, we love them and couldn't be happier for how they have turned their marriage around, but we aren't anything like them.

When Beth gets home from work, Bob has everything ready. The meal is cooked, the kid's homework is done, and the house isn't a wreck. When the kids are sick he's the one who takes care of them, which is just the opposite of what you'd think. He's incredibly patient, gentle, and giving. And, he's as feminine as they come.

At family gatherings Bob and I can catch up on family talk about who's doing what, but after that, nothing. Actually, that isn't completely true. He always wants to know about our ministry, and their financial support goes a long way. My point is that they are not a model for us to follow. I can't be like him, and Caroline can't be like Beth. For that matter, I can't be like Beth either. If anything, Caroline and Bob have the most in common, other than Bob being a better cook and more organized. Those are Caroline's words!

When we go down the list of couples we know, none are particularly appealing models for us to follow. Our friends are just as lost at this marriage stuff as we are. Family isn't a lot of help either, and we know too much about most of them anyhow. On top of that, the two of you have told us not to try and build a marriage like yours.

We talked about many of the Christian books on marriage that we have studied and how they were geared more towards the model of first century Roman culture, albeit a much kinder version. I'm not saying they weren't helpful, because we learned a lot from them. They did cover how we should act towards each other, but they didn't talk about exactly why it was so difficult to act the way we should. Concepts like sin nature, the flesh, and the self are thrown around and everyone nods their heads as though they understand what they are talking about. For us, many of those terms are too general and esoteric for practical guidance. What should we do day-to-day?

Some of the books emphasized that we should be imitators as the Apostle Paul writes in 1 Thessalonians 1:6-7.

> You became imitators of us and of the Lord, for you welcomed the message in the midst of severe suffering with the joy given by the Holy Spirit. 7 And so you became a model to all the believers in Macedonia and Achaia.

Your dozen or so email references to Romans 12:1-2 are finally sinking in. We are not against *imitating* as long as what is imitated emerges as a result of the same Holy Spirit in us who was in the Lord, and in Paul, and who raised Jesus from the dead.

All this time we have tried to produce from our flesh what can only be produced with the Holy Spirit. Even with all of that, we still feel like our marriage, and lives, are more often patterned after Romans 7:15, "I do not understand what I do. For what I want to do I do not do, but what I hate I do."

The problem is that when I am supposed to say something to Caroline as a loving and wise husband, where are the words I should choose? From whose lips have I heard them? Every skill I ever learned, I had experts to study and imitate. Where's the list of Spirit-filled options to study? Where are the experts to imitate? Where is the Pre-Fall Marriage Manual? Even with offering myself as a living sacrifice, I need practical and doable actions for living out the renewing of my mind. I get the idea of climbing up onto the altar, but at some point I have to roll down off of it and get on with my day.

Jack

Subject: Re: No Mentors to Follow

Jack and Caroline, this is Rick.

Stay on God's altar

I'm going to start with what you ended your last email. I don't think we have to get down off of God's altar to get on with our day. Our day can come to us as we maintain our position on His altar. Of course, the storms and waves of life can rage against us and wash us off in the way a person can be washed out of a lifeboat. And, when that happens, we have to get back onto the altar. For me, unfortunately, I don't need storms. My lack of focus and intentionality causes me to spend a lot more time off of the altar than I prefer. If I'm totally honest, it's the storms that cause me to return to the altar from which I wander away during good weather.

Beth and Bob

Beth and Bob do have a unique relationship. There's a lot you know about them, and I bet there's a lot you don't; especially about Bob. When we met them, Beth was finishing the final version of her second book on surgery, was on the editorial board of three surgery journals, and had just become the youngest full professor of surgery in the history of her institution. She was quite the powerhouse and often had the intense demeanor to go with it. When we asked Bob how he mustered the courage to ask her out he said, "It was simple; she asked me."

They were as opposite as two people can get. She was extroverted and he was introverted on his most outgoing day! She always knew what she wanted and he didn't care. It wasn't that he didn't care in the way some spouses don't care what the other wants. He didn't care in the sense that he was fine with whatever she wanted. He had no preferences. Unfortunately, he had lost his ability to sense his own desires and needs. He was everyone's servant, or as Beth used to say, "Everyone's doormat."

Bob was the youngest brother of four boys, and they gave him the nickname, "Little sister." They were all athletic, including his father and grandfather. He remembers being about eight years old when he, his father, and grandfather were throwing a baseball. His grandfather said, "Try throwing with your dominant hand." Bob's father said, "He is." Bob said the next hour of his grandfather's throwing lesson was excruciating and boring. He remembered thinking, "Why would anyone throw a ball to someone just to have it thrown back...over and over and over? Why not bake something everyone could enjoy?"

Bob was teased by other boys mercilessly in middle school and high school. His own brothers, unlike everyone else's brothers, wouldn't step in to defend him because they thought it would "make him tougher." He rarely got praise at home, even though he was a straight A student. His only friends were girls until they became preoccupied with their boyfriends. As a result, whatever Bob enjoyed didn't matter, whatever he did wasn't good enough, and whenever people got on with their "real" lives, he was left behind. That's why when Beth asked him out on a date he thought it was a joke. She told us that what attracted her to him was that she thought he was authentic, interesting, unique, and safe.

As you both know, Beth is All-Everything. Her weakest areas are exceptional by anyone's standards. That's why when she first approached us about working with them, I was stunned when she said, "I feel so inadequate when I am with him." I thought, "Inadequate? Really?" Beth said the real eye-opener was when their youngest daughter cut her finger on a sharp piece of plastic and ran right past her to Bob. Her child ran past a world-class surgeon and presented her finger to Bob!

The irony is that Bob had the same feelings of inadequacy in the presence of Beth and he thought his life was unimportant compared to hers. It never occurred to him that, at least for a small child with a cut finger, he was more adequate, important, and trusted than her mother who, if it had been cut off could have sewn it back on.

Beth and Bob's marriage began to turn around when they accepted each other's strengths, and appreciated each other's unique expression of Jesus. Beth studied Bob in exactly the same way she would learn a new surgical procedure. Rather than get caught up defending her own shortcomings, she observed exactly how he was safe and nurturing, and how he would be genuinely interested in what was important to others.

Beth noticed how Bob made eye contact with people and gave them his complete attention. He spoke slower and softer than she did. These were the very traits that kept her attracted to him when they were dating. He made her feel mentally and emotionally safe and nurtured. Their children also feel the same when they are with him. Her challenge was to grow in his strengths; not resent them.

It was in studying Bob that Beth realized the way he showed attention to others was no different than how she was attentive to her patients. She didn't have to learn anything new; she simply needed to focus her existing strength in a different direction.

Bob learned that it was okay for him to have preferences. He also accepted that his preferences could be good for their relationship in the same way as what we wrote about Caroline's desires and needs being what your relationship needed as well. Bob preferred quiet walks and Beth didn't realize how much she needed them in order to slow down and relax. She would repeatedly resist going on them, and then be glad she did.

Bob accepted the fact that the set of traits he possessed in order to reflect his image of Jesus to this world had been labeled by others as "feminine," and there was nothing he could do about it. Eventually, he embraced who he was, and decided there was nothing he wanted to do about it. He aligned himself with the declaration of Psalm 139:14, "I praise you because I am fearfully and wonderfully made; your works are wonderful, I know that full well."

Another breakthrough for Bob was in the importance of his life. In the past, he viewed himself through the same value system as his family viewed him. Men made money, played sports, shot animals, caught fish, and they most certainly did not pick up crying babies. That wasn't Bob. His athleticism was expressed by getting to a crying baby before any woman could, and his value in the lives of Beth and their children surpassed any financial measure. One night Beth looked him straight in the eyes and said,

> "You are an amazing surgeon because every operation
> I perform has your support. I could never have
> accomplished what I have without you."

Connecting

Another issue Bob and Beth had to deal with was the pattern of letting the urgent matters in her life dictate and crowd out how much time of hers was available to him. This led to bitterness and resentment by both of them. When Beth was available, he used his defense of pouting and withdrawing to try and make her feel bad because she wasn't giving him enough attention. This did not go well at all because Beth doesn't respond to that kind of baiting or punishment, and the type of attention he ended up receiving from her as a result was far from desirable.

When Beth releases her anger she can be more demeaning than anything Bob's brothers had to offer. That is partly why she felt so familiar to him. His Imago formed around his brothers with whom he longed to connect. The challenge was for Bob and Beth to heal and grow out of their destructive patterns.

Beth broke the pattern of Bob's abandonment feelings by becoming more intentional in setting aside time for him. They started by having a regular date night that Bob knew he could count on. And when she was with him, she was with him. No cell phone unless she was on call. No looking around the restaurant for people she knew. No wandering off in her head to plan what she would be working on later that night or the next day. When they were together, she was his and he was hers. Period.

Another key issue they had to deal with by establishing a new pattern was when Beth was upset about something, Bob would assume it was his fault. This caused him to feel and act intimidated. He'd usually ask, "Did I do something wrong? Are you mad at me?" She would become angrier because his insecurities and questions were a distraction from what was really bothering her. I remember their big breakthrough.

They were on our couch and we were talking about this pattern. Both of them were getting more and more frustrated. Finally, he turned to her and boldly proclaimed, "How about when you are mad, I'm just going to assume it's NOT about me unless you tell me otherwise?!" She paused, threw her hands up into the air and yelled, "THANK YOU!!! It was a beautiful moment. Now she has the freedom to be angry about other things without worrying about its impact on him or her having to deal with his insecurities. He has the freedom to not live with ongoing of anxiety when she is angry. Bob's hypersensitivity to her anger was frustrating and puzzling to them until they considered his childhood experiences.

Whenever Bob's brothers were mad about something, they would take it out on him. They would slap him around and then hold him down until he was furious. Sometimes they would even beat him with their fists. He couldn't tell anyone because he would be taunted even more, and rejected for being weak. What Bob and Beth assumed was his simple pattern of anxious hypersensitivity to her anger, was in reality his complex behavioral instinct for survival. Beth's anger would set off all of his triggers and defenses that were directly connected to the mental, emotional, and physical abused he endured at the hands of his brothers.

Patterned behaviors are a response and do not arise out of a void. There's a reason for everything we do; even if it makes no sense to anyone else, or even ourselves. When a patterned behavior gets in the way of something we want more, it is time to break the pattern and establish a new and more effective behavior. Bob was able to become bolder by considering how Beth handled conflicts.

At work, Beth is direct in asking questions to identify the cause of a conflict. She listens well and rarely gets emotional unless someone risks a patient's care and will not take responsibility to make sure it doesn't happen again. Bob learned that when he wasn't feeling like an intimidated child, he was fine with Beth's anger. He could ask direct and helpful questions without feeling anxious. His discomfort with her anger was not her fault. With her, he didn't need the triggers and defenses that he created for protection from his brothers. They only got in the way of what he wanted more, which was a great relationship with her.

Role models are all around us

So what does all of this have to do with your concern about the lack of role models for building a marriage? Bob and Beth were role models for each other, and they also realized there were role models all around them. Almost anyone could be their role model for something, no matter how small. Or, someone could be a role model for how not to do something.

Bob shared that one time he was having a beer with his father and said, "Dad, I'm glad I was part of your marriage to mom because I have learned what not to do." His dad took a long drink of beer, set his glass down, and stared directly at Bob for several seconds. That's when Bob realized his dad just might "rip his head off and never be convicted by a jury of his peers." His dad looked away for a moment and then back with a more understanding expression and said, "Bob, remember, there are a lot of ways to do something wrong."

It's interesting that you would ask about a Pre-Fall Marriage Manual because the Bible contains what we refer to as the Hidden Book of Marriage. It's getting late. I will write more about that later.

Blessings on your day,

Rick

Subject: Our Spouse as a Role Model and Changing Patterns

Rick and Georgeann, this is Jack.

I had no idea about Bob's childhood. I've only seen his family a handful of times, though it is apparent they are rough around the edges. "Little sister" though? That's just wrong. Almost as wrong as me looking down on his feminine side. Rather than feminine, I should say his, *more like Caroline's image of Jesus side.* And as for him rarely getting praise at home, that's what I lived. I've been doing to him in my mind exactly what was done to him by his family, and to me by mine. I've been judging him for who he wasn't created to be and I have not been appreciating him for who he is. I should claim Psalm 139:14 for him in my mind. "I praise you God because Bob is fearfully and wonderfully made; your works are wonderful, I know that full well."

It's crazy that Beth would feel inadequate when she compares herself to Bob, but I guess it's how she sees it that matters. It sounds just like her though to study Bob, or anyone else for that matter. Speaking of studying people, you got me curious. I have been watching Caroline.

Erica came in crying yesterday from playing with some girls in the village. She was crushed because they made fun of her. Caroline just held her and let her cry for a while. She asked Erica more about her feelings and what had happened. Eventually Erica calmed down and Caroline gave her a kiss and sent her back out. It was clear that Erica felt mentally and emotionally safe again. I so would have handled that differently.

I would have talked about the differences in our cultures, why people reject others who aren't like them, and blah blah blah blah blah. Caroline has pointed out several times in the past how I almost always try to treat emotional pain with intellectual explanations. Not sure why I am so different from her. When it comes to making people feel safe and nurtured, Bob and Caroline are so on the same page. Maybe Beth and I have more in common than I thought.

I completely agree with Beth acknowledging Bob's role in her success. Caroline and I talked last night about how much our success depends on each other. Our ministries are related, yet unique, and we both need each other to do our roles around the house.

We also talked about how we are changing. We seem to appreciate each other more than we used to, and we can talk without becoming defensive. In many ways it doesn't feel like we have changed all that much, but then again, we aren't arguing nearly as often as we used to. Working through these emails has been really helpful, but that doesn't explain all of it because we've talked through lots of other things that you haven't brought up. Please don't think we don't appreciate your efforts though, because we do.

One area in which we have made a lot of progress is in working together on Caroline's Bible studies for women in the village. When she used to ask me to look at them, I would come up with all sorts of "suggestions." I would try to convert her message to *my* voice with the objectives that I would have emphasized. Neither of us was wrong in our approach, but she would often get defensive and frustrated. During one confrontation in particular I snapped back at her with the question, "Do you want my opinion or just affirmation?!" She responded, "Both!"

Now, I ask her questions about what *she* wants to convey, and what *she* thinks the women are struggling with. I ask her questions about what God has been speaking to her when she studies the material. I help her discover the clarity that the Holy Spirit is already forming within her. When I ask her these questions it makes me think about how the study is relevant to me. The better I got at being genuinely curious about helping her and not dictating my perspective, the better she learned how to do the same for me. We finally trust each other with our creativity because we are getting more skillful and safer. Don't get me wrong, we aren't trying to be Holy Spirit substitutes for each other. It is more about assisting each other and reflecting back the wisdom God has given to each of us.

This is Caroline.

I jumped all over the idea about Beth giving Bob her undistracted time. Jack is an amazing thinker, and sometimes it takes a lot of effort for him to stay focused on us when we are on a date. What has helped is that we decide before the date what time the date will end. That way I know I have him until then, and he knows he can hold off his other thoughts until we are finished. Sometimes a date goes beyond our agreed upon time, but that usually means the date went really well. ☺☺

What helped us even more from your last email was the way Bob decided to handle Beth's anger. I can totally picture Beth throwing her hands up into the air and yelling, "THANK YOU!" When we read that we looked at each other, smiled, and broke out laughing.

When Jack appears to be mad about something, I have asked far too many times, "Is it me?" I know it stems from my insecurities and fear of abandonment. As a result, I often misinterpret Jack's intensity as anger. This insight will prevent many arguments that were going to happen in the future.

Three nights ago I pointed out to Jack that he must have been struggling with a decision or something because he was starting to pick at me for little things. I offered to help him figure out what was really bothering him. He totally denied it. Then last night he came into the kitchen, stood there for a moment and said, "You're right." I replied, "Of course I am. What about?" He said, "I do pick at you when I'm frustrated."

Praise God! Jack caught himself in the act right there in the kitchen and owned what he was getting ready to do. Now that he recognizes it, he says he can change his pattern. My expressing my need to feel safe and accepted was what helped him realize that this was an area in which he needed to grow. Way way cool! We rejoiced in our victory.

In closing, role models are all around us and it is our responsibility to perceive and incorporate what is helpful for our unique relationship. All we have to do is be intentional and communicate. Simple, but not easy.

We are both curious about this Hidden Book of Marriage. It appears to be hidden pretty well.

Good morning since you should be waking up in about an hour,

Caroline

Subject: Self-Judgment and the Strong Emotions of Others

Jack, this is Rick

Judging ourselves and others

Even after all of these years, I never cease to be amazed how courageous people are when I hear their story such as Bob's. It is so easy to think harshly of others when we don't have all of the facts. That is why God is the only One capable of judging accurately because He is the only One with all of the facts and the righteousness to do so. And, the most important fact of all is that Jesus died for our sins, and the sins of those people whom we don't understand. When I look back over my life, there isn't an increment of time small enough that would not declare me a sinner and worthy of judgment. I am comforted by the Apostle Paul's writing to the Corinthians.

> This, then, is how you ought to regard us: as servants of Christ and as those entrusted with the mysteries God has revealed. 2 Now it is required that those who have been given a trust must prove faithful. 3 I care very little if I am judged by you or by any human court; indeed, I do not even judge myself. 4 My conscience is clear, but that does not make me innocent. It is the Lord who judges me. 5 Therefore judge nothing before the appointed time; wait until the Lord comes. He will bring to light what is hidden in darkness and will expose the motives of the heart. At that time each will receive their praise from God. (1 Corinthians 4:1-5).

To me, this means that I have enough facts about myself to repent, but not enough to judge. I have to wait for the Lord to do that. And, I certainly don't have the right to judge my actions in the past based on the insight that I have now. That was then, and the blood of Christ was sufficient then. What happens now is now, and the blood of Christ is sufficient now.

Not having the right to judge does not mean, however, that we should not assess what is right or wrong, or deal appropriately with others when they sin against us or someone else. It just means we should not judge them for doing so because we are all capable of almost anything given the right circumstances.

Beth's feelings of inadequacy were based on her comparison of herself to Bob, and were the result of her self-directed judgment using her perception of Bob as the law. There's a lot of potential for breakdown in that type of system. Who do we choose to be the person to whom we compare ourselves? In what areas do we compare ourselves? It isn't fair to compare our inner-world to anyone's outer-world. Someone's outside *appearance* can be very different from their inside *experience*. Beth finally accepted our request: "Give to yourself no more and no less grace than you would to your child or your best friend."

It brings us great joy to hear that you and Caroline are able to help each other with your Bible studies. Indicators that safety and nurturing are at their highest is when people feel the freedom to bring out their creativity.

Treating emotional pain with intellectual explanations

Don't be too hard on yourself about Caroline's observation that you "almost always try to treat emotional pain with intellectual explanations." We can only offer others what we have. You were not taught how to process your emotions when you were young, so now you need to fill in that void by learning to do so. Once you learn how to experience, tolerate, and process your own emotions, you will be better able to do the same with the emotions of others.

For some Christians, experiencing the strong emotions of others is very uncomfortable. Their response is often to administer a quick intellectualized slap-a-verse answer that is more designed to soothe the uncomfortable feelings of the one offering the answer than the recipient. This attempt can be little more than, "Gee, your emotional wound and pain is gross and makes me feel bad. Let me slap this bandage verse on it. Now, go and act healed so I will feel better."

We are glad to hear how you two are appreciating each other more and more. Appreciation begins with understanding, and understanding begins with listening. It also brings us great joy to hear that the two of you have talked through many other issues than what we have written about. There is no single series of emails that can encompass all that God has for you, and if a single series could, we certainly are not qualified to write it.

Your marriage is the only one of its kind in all of human history and all of human future. We can only offer what is working for us after many decades of remodeling, and what we have seen work for others.

Caroline, this is Georgeann.

The much younger version of Rick and Jack have a lot in common. Having an approximate duration for any commitment like a date night is important to him. For years I just thought it was odd, and to some extent it is. He knows it. The important point is that we are all "odd" in our own ways, which is what makes us unique and "fearfully and wonderfully made." It's been said that we should only fight battles big enough to matter and small enough to win. I will fight actual sin and am content to leave "odd" alone.

I'm glad Beth's yelling, "THANK YOU!" spoke to you. Rick and I avoid the "Are you mad at me?" thing by giving an explicit warning. If I come home fuming about something I will start with, "I'm really mad and it's not at you!" He doesn't go as far as to throw up his hands and say, "Good!," but I can read it in his eyes.

Rick said to tell you he is working on an email about the Hidden Book of Marriage. I will give you a hint. The marriage relationship is the most intimate extension of a relationship between members of the Body of Christ.

You two are doing great work on yourselves and your marriage. We are proud of you.

In Him,

Georgeann

Subject: The Bible's Hidden Book of Marriage

Jack and Caroline, this is Rick.

Submit to each other out of reverence for Christ

The Bible is a book about relationships that includes our relationships with one another and our personal relationship with God. It speaks to us from a Post-Fall perspective about how to interact with strangers, neighbors, family, enemies, friends, employers, fellow Christians, husbands, wives, slaves, children, and even ourselves. Wives, along with slaves and children in the New and Old Testament fall under the category of property.

It is clear in Genesis 3:16 that from a Post-Fall perspective of marriage, husbands were given rule over wives. '"To the woman he said, "I will make your pains in childbearing very severe; with painful labor you will give birth to children. Your desire will be for your husband, and he will rule over you."'

Even so, in Ephesians Chapter 5 the Apostle Paul portrays a husband's rule as one of love, sacrifice, and mutual submission in the context of verse 21,

"Submit to one another out of reverence for Christ."

Three times he tells husbands to love their wives. The first is in verse 25,

"Husbands, love your wives, just as Christ loved the church and gave himself up for her"

The second is in verse 28,

"In this same way, husbands ought to love their wives as their own bodies. He who loves his wife loves himself."

And the third is in verse 33,

"However, each one of you also must love his wife as he loves himself, and the wife must respect her husband."

Yet in the face of these three *love your wife* directives, some men cling singularly to verses 22 and 23,

> "Wives, submit yourselves to your own husbands as you do to the Lord. 23 For the husband is the head of the wife as Christ is the head of the church, his body, of which he is the Savior."

There is often a complete distortion by men of what "husband is the head of the wife" means, particularly when exercised in the absence of the love for their wife that Paul intended. These men reinforce their dominance with 1 Corinthians 14:34 where Paul writes, "Women should remain silent in the churches. They are not allowed to speak, but must be in submission, as the law says." If I remember correctly, Jack, you asked about this verse in a previous email.

While Paul's writings do not unambiguously advocate the Pre-Fall perspective of Adam and Eve ruling coequally in the garden, we think he comes as close as he can within the context of his culture.

Paul's commanding a man to love his wife at that time was the equivalent of commanding him to love his property such as a dog or a blanket. This would have been especially strange to his male readers since a common Jewish prayer for males in leadership was to thank God they were not born a woman. In essence, Paul is saying to love and submit to this woman whom you own, and whom you thank God every day you were not born to be.

What I have just written about the radical nature of Paul's directive was influenced by an excellent sermon I recently heard on Ephesians 5:21-33. It is titled, the Spirit-filled Marriage (I Believe in the Church, pt. 10) by Josh Miller at Harvest Vineyard Church in Ames, Iowa. If you ever get a good internet connection, here's the link to the podcast

https://www.harvestvc.org/sermonaudiorss.xml.

The sermon starts at the 9 minute mark. I'll try to get a copy of the text and send it to you.

Jack,

A while back you wrote,

> The problem is that when I am supposed to say something to Caroline as a loving and wise husband, where are the words I should choose? From whose lips have I heard them? Every skill I ever learned, I had experts to study and imitate. Where's the list of Spirit-filled options to study? Where are the experts to imitate? Where is the Pre-Fall Marriage Manual?

Specific guidance for a Pre-Fall Marriage

The specific guidance you are looking for on how to live out a Pre-Fall Marriage has been in front of you for your entire Christian life. It is the same guidance that the Bible offers on how we as Christians should interact with one another and those around us. As Georgeann hinted in her last email, this is based on the premise that a marriage relationship between Christians is the most intimate extension of being members of the Body of Christ.

This intimate extension means that the marriage relationship not only *encompasses* how you and Caroline should relate to each other as Christians, it also provides for an exclusive and even greater connection of intimacy between the two of you as spouses. We refer to this as, "Yes, and even more." Yes, Scripture applies to your relationship as individual believers, and even more as spouses.

As a husband, I think God wants me to treat Georgeann at least as well and even better than I treat anyone else, and I think He wants her to do the same with me. Therefore, Scriptures that say I should love my enemies, such as Luke 6:27 could be appended with, "… and love Georgeann with the same love as what I am commanding you to have for your enemies, and even more." Scriptures that say I should speak the truth in love (Ephesians 4:15), could be appended with, "…and speak the truth to Georgeann with the same love that you should have for a fellow believer, and even more." Personalizing Scripture in this way does not diminish its truth as long as the original meaning is preserved.

I'm not advocating altering verses to create separate versions of the Bible such as the RRV, GRV, JRV, and CRV. You know, the Rick Revised Version, Georgeann Revised Version, Jack Revised Version, and Caroline Revised Version. Besides, it would be really confusing for Bob and Beth.

Here's two of my favorite passages for showing you what I mean about finding specific guidance from God on His will for living out our marriage. I use the word "favorite" in the most *unable to perform and fall short of every day* way.

Before I do, however, there's a big difference between *personalizing* Scripture to build and strengthen a marriage, and *deliberately distorting* Scripture to establish and preserve an abuser's dominance. For example, let's look at the greatest commandment.

> Hearing that Jesus had silenced the Sadducees, the Pharisees got together. 35 One of them, an expert in the law, tested him with this question: 36 "Teacher, which is the greatest commandment in the Law?"

> 37 Jesus replied: "'Love the Lord your God with all your heart and with all your soul and with all your mind.' 38 This is the first and greatest commandment. 39 And the second is like it: 'Love your neighbor as yourself.' 40 All the Law and the Prophets hang on these two commandments." (Matthew 22:34-40)

If I was an abusive husband, my deliberate distortion for Georgeann would be:

> Jesus replied: "'Love **Rick** with all your heart and with all your soul and with all your mind.' 38 This is the first and greatest commandment. 39 And the second is like it: 'Love **Rick** as yourself.' 40 All the Law and the Prophets hang on these two commandments." (Matthew 22:37-40, AbuserRV)

It would not be appropriate for Georgeann to love me with all of her heart and with all of her soul and with all of her mind because those should only be directed in that way towards God. It is fine, however, for Georgeann to direct verse 39 towards me. In my case the personalization of verse 39 would be, "Rick, love **Georgeann** as yourself. This makes sense to us because Georgeann and I should love each other even more than we would any neighbor.

The following two examples are types of verses that Josh Miller refers to as the "one anothers."

'"A new command I give you: Love **one another**. As I have loved you, so you must love **one another**."' (John 13:34)

Jack, if Jesus was speaking to you about your marriage he could just as easily have said,

"A new command I give you: Love Caroline. As I have loved you, so you must love Caroline.

If He was speaking to Caroline it would be,

"A new command I give you: Love Jack. As I have loved you, so you must love Jack.

The second example is,

"By this everyone will know that you are my disciples, if you love **one another**." (John 13:35)

Using the singular form of disciples, your version becomes,

"By this everyone will know that you are my disciple, if you love Caroline."

And Caroline's version becomes,

"By this everyone will know that you are my disciple, if you love Jack."

For me and Georgeann, this means that according to Jesus, the evidence of me being His disciple is weakened if I do not love Georgeann. And, her evidence of being His disciple is weakened if she does not love me.

Personalizing verses that can relate to marriage make it much more difficult for us to gloss over them as just theoretical or intellectual suggestions. It makes them real in our daily experience of how we should relate to each other.

Now let's look at Luke Chapter 6 again for a very uncomfortable reality about loving my enemies and loving Georgeann if she would behave like one.

> "But to you who are listening I say: Love your enemies, do good to those who hate you, [28] bless those who curse you, pray for those who mistreat you. [29] If someone slaps you on one cheek, turn to them the other also. If someone takes your coat, do not withhold your shirt from them. [30] Give to everyone who asks you, and if anyone takes what belongs to you, do not demand it back. [31] Do to others as you would have them do to you.
>
> [32] "If you love those who love you, what credit is that to you? Even sinners love those who love them. [33] And if you do good to those who are good to you, what credit is that to you? Even sinners do that. [34] And if you lend to those from whom you expect repayment, what credit is that to you? Even sinners lend to sinners, expecting to be repaid in full. [35] But love your enemies, do good to them, and lend to them without expecting to get anything back. Then your reward will be great, and you will be children of the Most High, because he is kind to the ungrateful and wicked. [36] Be merciful, just as your Father is merciful. (Luke 6:27-36)

If Jesus wants me to love my enemies and do good to those who hate me (Luke 6:27), then I am to love Georgeann and do good to her, even if she hates me, or snaps at me, or withdraws from me, or does anything that hurts my feelings, or acts like anyone who has hurt my feelings in the past, or has inconvenienced me, or does not anticipate my slightest desire. Notice the progression from hate to perceived trivial slight.

I am to be an intentional giver of my love to Georgeann, not an entitled consumer of hers. Loving Georgeann in the way Jesus calls me to love her is difficult, even when she is loving in return, let alone if she would hate me. No matter what, God calls me to love her. And, He calls her to love me.

Abusive relationships

This begs the question, however, how long should someone stay with an abusive spouse who is mentally, emotionally, spiritually, and/or physically dangerous. I have no single answer. Each person in this type of relationship needs to seek God for clear direction on whether to stay or leave in the power of the Holy Spirit.

Abusers who profess to be a Christian often like to proclaim that "God hates divorce." I am pretty sure that if God hates divorce, which He does, He hates even more the behaviors that lead to it. God's heart is not to collude with an abuser by holding one spouse down with His Word, while the other torments him or her by continually and intentionally inflicting mental, emotional, spiritual, and/or physical harm.

As I write this, the difficulty of applying any Scripture to a hurting marriage weighs heavily. Our only hope begins with what we have written many times before, Romans 12:1-2.

> Therefore, I urge you, brothers and sisters, in view of God's mercy, to offer your bodies as a living sacrifice, holy and pleasing to God—this is your true and proper worship. 2 Do not conform to the pattern of this world, but be transformed by the renewing of your mind. Then you will be able to test and approve what God's will is—his good, pleasing and perfect will.

And carrying out "his good, pleasing and perfect will" can only happen if we are in relationship with Him as described in Philippians 2:12-13.

> Therefore, my dear friends, as you have always obeyed—not only in my presence, but now much more in my absence—continue to work out your salvation with fear and trembling, 13 for it is God who works in you to will and to act in order to fulfill his good purpose.

I will close with three cautions about personalizing these types of verses to a marriage relationship.

First, I offer this creative application of Scripture to you as guidance for discovering God's original will for your marriage, and not as an attempt to change the meaning of any verse. I encourage the two of you to discover which verses are helpful for building your marriage.

Second, converting verses about how Christians should behave towards one another into specific statements about your marriage relationship must not be used for manipulation.

And third, be discerning when anyone interprets Scripture because abusers, or even those who are sincerely wrong, can distort anything to suit their purpose.

I know this email went long, but it was important to develop this idea as fully as I could. Let me know your thoughts when you get a chance.

In Him,

Rick

Subject: Re: The Bible's Hidden Book of Marriage

Rick and Georgeann, this is Caroline.

Jack is traveling again, though we did get a chance to read your last email before he left.

Specific guidance for a Pre-Fall marriage

It caught us totally off guard that you and Georgeann are telling us that what Scripture says about Christians loving one another as the Body of Christ applies even more to a marriage relationship. We talked about this for hours. The implication is that God's Pre-Fall will for living out a marriage is revealed in His Redeemed Church. He redeemed His Church and the implementation of marriage at the same time and in the same way through Jesus. This transcends any cultural view of marriage. According to this perspective, everything about marriage between the Fall and Jesus' resurrection was the same detour under the law that we all experienced individually.

We have listened to the traditional teaching of, *wives submit to your husband's desires without regard for your own*, forever. Even though we wanted to be obedient to God, that perspective just didn't feel right to either of us and seemed out of balance with the rest of Scripture. The message was, "Oh you wives are very very special. You are the most special servants of all."

On the one hand, the Church is the Body of Christ and everyone should love and serve one another. Sounds great! On the other hand, wives, shut up and serve your husband. What?! Why the double standard? According to that model, I would rather be Jack's brother in Christ than his wife! Though for various reasons we are both glad I am not.

Transitioning and maturing of Church culture

As Jack and I were talking about this last night it occurred to me that adding this new perspective for applying Scripture brings a different kind of transitioning in the Bible; a transitioning of culture.

The first transition we all go through is as an individual who is alienated from God, and then accepts Jesus as Savior to become a member of the Body of Christ. This other transition I am thinking about is the maturing of the Body of Christ over thousands of years in how it interprets and applies Scripture. I get how unsettling this thought of a maturing Church can be, but I think we are all glad to be beyond the eras of the Crusades, Inquisition, and when Scripture was used by some to justify slavery.

This is fresh in our minds because we had a couple from a different mission group over for dinner last weekend and this topic came up. We struggled with two questions in particular.

1) Does the Church change the culture, or does culture change the Church?

2) Is the expression of Church influenced by what culture is willing to tolerate, or is the expression of culture influenced by what the Church is willing to approve?

Our answer to each question was, "Yes and Yes" for varying times in Church history.

Caroline and Jack's hidden verses

Jack and I are both teaching out of Romans and when we were reading your email at the kitchen table, a couple of verses came to mind. I thought of Romans 13:8,

> Let no debt remain outstanding, except the continuing debt to love **one another**, for whoever loves others has fulfilled the law.

My version became,

> Let no debt remain outstanding, except the continuing debt to love **Jack**, for whoever loves others has fulfilled the law.

I also came up with Romans 14:13,

> Therefore let us stop passing judgment on **one another**. Instead, make up your mind not to put any stumbling block or obstacle in **the way of a brother or sister**.

It became,

> Therefore, Caroline, stop passing judgment on **Jack**. Instead, make up your mind not to put any stumbling block or obstacle in **Jack's way**.

In typical Jack form he came up with Romans 16:16,

> Greet **Jack** with a holy kiss. All the churches of Christ send greetings.

I smiled and came back with Romans 12:16,

> Live in harmony with **Jack**. Do not be proud, but be willing to associate with people of low position. Do not be conceited.

He returned my smile along with a series of wrestling moves that gently put me into a "low position" on our kitchen floor. My cooperative resistance ended up knocking over a chair. That woke Erica and Billy who came running out of their room. It felt good to have the kind of "fight" we were happy for our children to hear. They stood there for a moment and I yelled, "Help Mommy!" They immediately came running and piled onto Jack. ☺☺☺☺

Not sure when Jack will be back. This trip involves something he dislikes even more than donkeys...canoes!

Hope you two are doing well,

Caroline

P.S. A copy of the text of Josh's sermon would be great. We tried to listen online, but our connection kept failing. All we know for sure is that the first eight minutes are really good. ☺

Subject: Re: Re: The Bible's Hidden Book of Marriage

Caroline, this is Georgeann.

Transitioning and maturing of Church culture

Interesting thought about the transitioning and maturing of the Church. This also captures what happens in each of us. When Rick and I look back on our early years as Christians, we see how simplistic we were in some of our initial views. We were naive and took in whatever people told us about Church, God, the Holy Spirit, and faith.

I remember one day when Rick came across John 14:12 where Jesus said,

> "Very truly I tell you, whoever believes in me will do the works I have been doing, and they will do even greater things than these, because I am going to the Father."

Rick asked me, "Where are these 'greater things'? Why haven't I seen any?" He went down to our local Christian bookstore and asked a clerk the same questions. After reading several books, listening to excellent teachers, studying Scripture for ourselves, and experiencing the moving of the Holy Spirit, we matured in our thinking and began seeing and participating in some of these "greater things." They are not the foundation for our faith, rather, they are the fruit of our foundation in Jesus by the power of the Holy Spirit.

Each of us is a separate version

In Rick's last email about inserting our spouse's name in the "one another" verses, he wrote that he wasn't advocating a "separate version" of the Bible for each of us. While the idea of having a "separate version" is obviously foolish, it is true that each of us is a "separate version" when it comes to our faith and relationship with God.

Each of us has our own unique relationship with God along with our own personal faith and system of beliefs. Even though a group of Christians may believe in the Apostles' Creed or share a Tenets of Faith, every individual in that group is unique. Even though God is God, and there is only one God, we each have our own perceived image of Him and His character. We each have our own inner belief system that emphasizes our own personal values and the living out of those values. We each also have our own doubts and the living out of those as well. When you combine your image of God with your belief system and doubts, you are a unique worshiping human being who is unlike anyone who has ever lived, or ever will. This is what makes each of us uniquely special in our relationship with Him.

All of us are also unique in the way God plays His character through us like a song to a listening and watching world. Your song and Jack's song are different from the songs that He plays through me and Rick. This is why Rick and I try hard to respect each other's song of transitioning and maturing as we heal and grow.

Blind spots

Any song under development changes over time in the hands of the composer. It is the same for people who are healing and growing. That is why when it comes to what we have written in this series of emails, we know we have blind spots. The problem with our blind spots, however, is that we can't see them.☺ Perhaps the biggest problem with blind spots is when we are completely convinced that they cannot be there and we believe we are seeing perfectly. Not seeing Pre-Fall Marriage was our most recent blind spot. I'm sure we have more.

Church and culture

Your conversation with friends about the impact of the Church and culture on each other sounds interesting. We've seen those conversations range anywhere from enlightening and intriguing to confrontational and dogmatic. Some are even a reenactment of unholy wars. We all believe we are speaking the truth in love, but the best we can really do is speak *our* truth in love as we understand it. Whenever someone we are working with boldly says, "I just tell it like it is!" Rick is quick to point out,

> "No, you tell it like *you think* it is. I see things as *I think*
> they are, and you see things as *you think* they are. Only
> God knows how things *really are*. He is the only One
> who can tell it like it is."

Spouses who finally accept this observation will begin a potentially inflammatory comment with a qualifier such as, "From my perspective..." or "You may have a different opinion, but the way I see it is..." or "Correct me if I am wrong, but..." This approach restrains bias and dogmatism and makes room for alternate ideas and their communication.

You really had us laughing with "Greet Jack with a holy kiss" and "associate with people of low position." We still smile when we picture the four of you wrestling on your kitchen floor.

In Him,

Georgeann

P.S. Josh sent us his notes. Rick is listening to the sermon again, and editing them into a more readable form. He said he will be finished in a day or two. He likes doing this sort of thing. I'm pretty sure that someday he wants to be a writer. If he ever does, there will be several high school English teachers rolling over in their graves because he always got Cs and Ds. Even so, you never know what God can do.

Subject: Marriage Sermon on Ephesians 5:21-33 by Josh Miller

Jack and Caroline, this is Rick.

I finally finished converting Pastor Josh's sermon notes. This isn't a word-for-word transcript, but it is very close.

Some of his main points are:

1) Wives are not told to subordinate themselves to their husband as the unquestioned king of his castle.

2) Paul calls for mutual submission between husbands and wives, and gentleness with children, which was counter cultural at the time.

3) Paul pulls back power and control from men, and replaces it with servanthood and love.

4) A husband should nourish and cherish his wife; not be an emotional brute.

5) A husband's godly love is not about ruling or commanding.

6) If your husband loves you, let him love you well and align with his love in the same way the Church is asked to align itself with Jesus and His love.

7) Most women are terrified to fully surrender their heart to a man because of abuse, arrogance, distortion, superiority, hierarchy, or patriarchy. These are fruit of the Fall.

8) Most men struggle with how to be a man; a strong, humble, tender, mature, secure, and loving man.

9) A Christian marriage should tell the same relationship story of Jesus and the Church. This means that people who see your marriage should take note and wonder why it is different. In this way, a marriage can point to the love of God and the power of the Holy Spirit.

Josh's Sermon

Good morning Church,

We have been working our way through the New Testament book of Ephesians this Fall. The first half of Ephesians is filled with wonderful theology about who God is and who we are when we are connected with Christ. The second half of the book is about *living out* our new identity in Christ. It is about how the life of God within us is lived out practically.

In the section of Ephesians, Chapter 5 verses 21 through 33, we are looking at today, we see how the life of the Holy Spirit in us is lived out within a Christian marriage. In our church we have people who are single, married, divorced, and widowed. Wherever we currently are, we have been profoundly shaped by the marriages around us. And, most of us have either experienced first-hand or witnessed the deep joy and richness, or the incredible pain marriage can bring.

Today, what I want you to do with me is to ask, "What if God, as the author of marriage, has something to say to me about this?" And, "What if God has something different for me than I might expect?"

> Prayer: We thank you God that we get to be your dearly loved people. We thank you today for your transforming power in our lives - you make everything new. We thank you that because Jesus Christ is raised from the dead, we can have hope for today and tomorrow. We are heading into a huge topic. We all come from different experiences - we have different things that get triggered. We submit to you our thoughts, feelings, and the previous theology we bring to the table. Apart from your wisdom about marriage, we are in trouble. We must have your heart and perspective. Would you shine your light on us and this topic today? For those who are hurting because of brokenness around marriage, hold and comfort them today. For married couples, encourage and give them hope. For singles, whether or not you ever lead them

into marriage, we honor and bless them this morning and their place in our church family. In the name of Jesus we pray. Amen.

To singles: We are talking about marriage today because it comes up next in Ephesians 5. I just want to say something out loud here...Singleness is not the waiting room for the main event, which for some is marriage and children. That is a satanic lie to keep you distracted and disoriented. Singleness is the opportunity to live a powerfully <u>Christ-like life of other-centered love</u> starting right now, and that is what I am praying for every person I know who is single.

Let's read the passage together.

21 Submit to one another out of reverence for Christ.

22 Wives, submit yourselves to your own husbands as you do to the Lord. 23 For the husband is the head of the wife as Christ is the head of the church, his body, of which he is the Savior. 24 Now as the church submits to Christ, so also wives should submit to their husbands in everything.

25 Husbands, love your wives, just as Christ loved the church and gave himself up for her 26 to make her holy, cleansing her by the washing with water through the word, 27 and to present her to himself as a radiant church, without stain or wrinkle or any other blemish, but holy and blameless. 28 In this same way, husbands ought to love their wives as their own bodies. He who loves his wife loves himself. 29 After all, no one ever hated their own body, but they feed and care for their body, just as Christ does the church - 30 for we are members of his body. 31 "For this reason a man will leave his father and mother and be united to his wife, and the two will become one flesh." 32 This is a profound mystery - but I am talking about Christ and the church. 33 However, each one of you also must love his wife as he loves himself, and the wife must respect her husband. (Ephesians 5:21-33)

I want to begin today with a couple of comments.

First, part of the framework for understanding this section of Ephesians is to remember that it is written TO and FOR Christians who are filled with the Holy Spirit. This is TO and FOR people who have the life of God in them and who the Apostle Paul just encouraged to go on being filled with the power and life of the Holy Spirit. It is only when filled with, and depending on the power and the life of the Holy Spirit, that any husband or wife can walk this out.

This is not a random talk about marriage. This is not Paul doing a Q & A with a group from a church plant talking about marriage. This is the gospel, inside of marriage, being filled with the Holy Spirit, in the context of a larger narrative of redemption and a larger teaching to a church community.

Next, many people see the words "head" and "'submit," in this passage and say, "What we need is a restoration of Christian marriage." What that means to them is that wives need to learn how to subordinate themselves to the needs of their husbands. And, that a well-run Christian family is one where the husband is the never challenged and unquestioned king of the castle.

This passage is a LOT more challenging than that oversimplification. Paul never says, "By head this is what I mean." If you do even a little bit of reading or research about this, you will find that there is a down-right battle about what these words mean.

The word translated "head"' is kephale, which can have multiple meanings.

One: "Head" means leader/ruler/governor - to be the head means to lead, rule, or govern.

Another: "Head" in ancient Greek means source. When ancient Greek writers would talk about headwaters of rivers, they would use this word as the source.

Still another: "Head" means the most prominent part - not leader/ruler/governor.

Paul has already used this word in two of those three ways in Ephesians alone.

A little more background - Paul is not instructing the Church in a vacuum. It was a fully patriarchal society. In their society, women were disdained and seen as inferior to men in every way. In Jewish culture, male Jewish leaders would literally pray a prayer every day thanking God that they were not born a woman. Women did not have legal standing and could not be witnesses in court; they were their husbands' possession. Greek culture was even worse. Fidelity was a concept that barely existed and if it did, was primarily for the sake of passing on male children to continue the family line.

Female babies were abandoned far more frequently than male, and were often raised to be prostitutes. Greek men married women with a massive age disparity, and husbands ruled the public sphere. It was an assumption in Greek and Jewish culture that women were not equals to men. That is the context Paul is speaking into.

In the ancient Greco-Roman world, philosophers used to instruct families about how they should live. They had what was called 'household codes.' Depending upon which school you belonged, these codes would be different. They taught about relationships between husbands and wives, parents and children, and masters and servants. With regard to household codes, all philosophers were in agreement that husbands were to rule their wives and everything else.

The apostle Paul is writing a household code for the Church in Ephesus in Ephesians Chapter 5 and the first part of Chapter 6. He is speaking into the cultural and sociological framework of his day, and he is using the form of household code that was familiar to ancient Greek writers: Husband/wife, parent/child, and master/slave. Paul even uses some of the same words: such as head and submit. His code also takes into account how Jesus Christ being raised from the dead constituted a new humanity, and how that should effect what was happening relationally in the Church on a day-to-day basis.

During this same time period, Caesar Augustus, who instituted the Pax Romana, put fines in place for people who stayed single too long, and he had hefty fines for divorce because the empire was falling apart at the seams. Any religion that was seen as dismantling the historic household codes was treated with great suspicion, and as a threat to the empire. And it is important to remember that Paul is writing while in Roman custody as he articulates the call of marriage inside the Church. His challenge is to uphold the best in traditional ancient values, while adapting and even subverting oppressive household codes.

Household codes normally instructed the male householder how to rule, yet Paul begins and ends his with mutual submission. He calls for gentleness with children, and instructs husbands on how to love their wives, not rule over them. This was absolutely counter-cultural at the time.

I want us to see how Paul taught God's word into that cultural framework and brought a compelling vision of marriage that is super relevant to us.

I will speak to three main areas: Sacrificial Love, Sanctifying Love, and Satisfying Love.

Marriage in this section of Ephesians is framed by mutual submission.

> [21] Submit to one another out of reverence for Christ.
> (Ephesians 5:21)

Everything that comes in verses 22 through 33 is to be viewed through the lens of Spirit-filled mutual submission. The big issue is about <u>both men and women</u> learning to submit to one another out of their reverence for Christ.

The challenge we have in our culture is that marriage is rarely viewed as the giving up of my own rights for the sake of you. Marriage, for too many, is about getting MY needs met. We have a very relationally transactional culture. Concepts such as *self-denial* and *preferring others above yourself* seem absolutely crazy.

There is an EXTREME command of mutuality here, giving to one another by way of a reciprocal submission; a Spirit-filled submission that is mutual in the Church.

Marriage is not an 'arms-folded' posture of, "This better be good..." Or, "When YOU start, I'll start." It is a mutual submission and abandoning to one another. In the 1st century, men would have heard this language and left church with their heads spinning! What are you talking about? My wife is my property; my possession. She is certainly not an equal or someone to whom I have to submit.

Paul doesn't just teach mutuality of husbands and wives in Ephesians. In 1 Corinthians he says that husbands and wives are not only equals, but their <u>bodies</u> belong to each other. They are equal partners in every area. Christian marriage is not about one person having authority over another - it is about mutual submission TO one another in the way God has created us.

But, being equal, doesn't mean men and women are interchangeable. There are ways that require submission to be lived out that fit men or women.

Let's look at Spirit-filled submission for husbands.

In the 1st century Greco-Roman culture, it was <u>counter-cultural to the extreme</u> to limit the amount of power a man had over his wife, children, and slaves. In each sphere of household authority, the Apostle Paul is pulling back power and control, and replacing it with <u>servanthood</u> and <u>love</u>. He is saying, "Inside the Christian Church there is a place of honor for women and children, even if there is not space for that in the culture."

What does <u>men</u> submitting to women look like in marriage?

#1 Sacrificial Love - a husband sacrifices his ego and selfishness to love his wife.

> Husbands, love your wives, just as Christ loved the church and gave himself up for her... (Ephesians 5:25)

For any of us husbands, our call is to sacrificially love our wives in ways that model or reflect the way Jesus loved the church.

A couple examples of this:

Jesus had a <u>pursuing</u> love...repeatedly going after outsiders to make them insiders. And, those who were caught in sin, to extend grace to them. His love was proactive.

Jesus loved with a <u>serving</u> love. One time the disciples were arguing about who was the greatest, and Jesus ended up disrobing and washing everyone's feet. Serving love looks like coming home and seeing dishes in the sink and realizing they are not self-cleaning! Someone needs to clean these dishes and that someone is me.

Jesus had a <u>burden-bearing</u> love. He died to take on the sins of other people. He takes things that weren't his fault or responsibility onto him and bears the burden to give us the gift of life. Paul says, husbands, treat your wife this way. Jesus literally gave His life to His own harm. Why is this so difficult for husbands? The instinct of every man is to be selfish and entitled.

The question for a husband should not be, "How do I get my needs met by this woman?" The question should be the opposite in, "How do I meet the needs of this woman?" We are to learn from Jesus how to reorient our hearts and submit our egos, desires, and ambition to sacrificially love our wives and make sure that they prosper and flourish.

#2 Sanctifying Love – a husband helps his wife reach her redemptive potential

> [26] to make her holy, cleansing her by the washing with water through the word, [27] and to present her to himself as a radiant church, without stain or wrinkle or any other blemish, but holy and blameless. (Ephesians 5:26-27)

When a woman chooses to marry a godly man, the result means she should reach more of her redemptive potential in large part BECAUSE she is married to this man - not in spite of being married to him.

Men, if we get married, the question concerning our goals should not be, "How can I serve God, live out my call, and get this woman to help me?" Rather, our goal should be, "Now that I am serving God, part of my call is to help this woman reach her full redemptive potential; making her holy, blameless, and radiant! Our goal should be to present our wives in all of their splendor to anyone around.

This is what Jesus does for the Church. This begins when He sees us; takes us out of sin, darkness, and shame; makes us a new creation; fills us with the Holy Spirit; gifts us; makes us his sons and daughters; and releases us into the world to participate with him in the renewal of all things. His goal is to present us as His bride without spot or blemish, and radiant!

An example of how Jesus relates to the church is in Hebrews 7:25. It says that Jesus *always lives to intercede for us*. One way we express sanctifying love to our wife is by constantly praying for her. We can pray blessing into her life; that God would lighten her load; that she would be filled with joy; full of faith and grace; that God would protect her; and that the kingdom would come more fully in her life. Which one of you wives wouldn't want a man to do that?

Sanctifying love draws our wife toward reaching her full redemptive potential. Many things fall into this category including the desires of her heart, her gifts, her career and vocational calling, and her dreams. How do I bring sanctifying love to bear on our marriage? I've only been married for 18 years so I feel like I'm just getting started. But I want to love Cory with a sanctifying love - like Christ loves me.

#3 Satisfying Love – a husband nourishes and cherishes his wife

> 28 In this same way, husbands ought to love their wives as their own bodies. He who loves his wife loves himself. 29 After all, no one ever hated their own body, but they feed and care for their body, just as Christ does the church— 30 for we are members of his body. 31 "For this reason a man will leave his father and mother and be united to his wife, and the two will become one flesh." (Ephesians 5:28 - 31)

Where it says 'feed and care for,' other translations say, "He will nourish and cherish." Men in a Christian marriage are not to be emotional brutes. Rather, they should learn how to nourish and cherish their wives. This is something we need to learn from Jesus and other men who do this for their wives.

Husbands, where there have been words of accusation, we are to speak words of LIFE. Where there have been words of despair, we are to speak words of HOPE. Satisfying love nourishes and cherishes. A good barometer would be to honestly ask your wife, "On a scale of 1 to 10, how cherished or nourished do you feel from me?" And then listen to her honest answer. Then ask, "What can I do to make you feel more cherished and nourished?" These actions aren't meant to create some type of legalism; rather, they are concrete meaningful ways to live out our love for our wife.

Spirit-filled mutual submission for husbands means we submit our egos, desires, and ambition to the prospering and flourishing of our wives, and cherish them during the process. We DO NOT get this vision of marriage from our culture, or most of our families.

If you are engaging at any level as a husband, or are soon to be one, this should cause you to ask, "How do I do that?" You have the Holy Spirit in you, which is the presence and power of God. That's how you do it. The Holy Spirit is good at this kind of loving. We learn to defer to him and let him live his life out through us toward our wives!

Let's move to Spirit-filled submission for wives.

> 22 Wives, submit yourselves to your own husbands as you do to the Lord. 23 For the husband is the head of the wife as Christ is the head of the church, his body, of which he is the Savior. 24 Now as the church submits to Christ, so also wives should submit to their husbands in everything. (Ephesians 5:22-24)

How do wives live in mutual submission? What is being asked here?

#1 Submit to their husband's love. Submit means 'to align yourself under something, line up underneath.' What is the wife lining up underneath? This passage doesn't talk about ruling or commanding at all! The only thing the husband has been commanded to do is to DIE in order to present his wife in splendor.

I think Paul is saying, wives, you are called to <u>let your husband love you well</u>. This is what submission is. Align under your husband's love as he does that. We could talk for 20 extra minutes about this, but isn't submitted alignment what the church needs to learn to do with Jesus? To submit to Him and <u>let Him love us well</u> as we align under his love. We know in our heads he loves us, but it is much tougher to receive and submit to his love in and out of every season of life.

My observations and experience has been that most women are terrified of fully surrendering their heart to another person. Because of the abuses of patriarchy, and how some Christian men have often been arrogant and misrepresented these verses, women often hold something back. This is a fruit of the Fall.

In Genesis 1 and 2, God created man and woman. They were totally equal and given the same commands. Sin entered the world along with something we call 'the Fall.' Sin and the Fall began the distortions and destructive superiority in relationships.

> Genesis 3:16 says, '"I will make your pains in childbearing very severe; with painful labor you will give birth to children. Your desire will be for your husband, and he will rule over you."

Many scholars interpret the word "desire" to mean that Eve will strive to have mastery over her husband. Why would she want this? I think the answer is to guard her heart and protect herself. There is nothing more terrifying than letting a man see you for who you are because he has the chance to reject you for who you are…which is why as I said before, some women often hold back.

I remember early in our marriage we were two broken people trying to love each other, and I can remember me thinking, "Why won't you let me love you?!" My wife is an incredibly strong woman, and it has taken years for her to say, "I trust that you're going to love me and I can line up under your love. And, I will let you serve me." THAT is a profound place to be. The call to mutual submission for a wife is to line up under her husband who is sacrificial in his sanctifying and satisfying love for her.

#2 Respect her husband

The only other specific thing mentioned for women in this passage is, "respect her husband."

> 33 However, each one of you also must love his wife as he loves himself, and the wife must respect her husband. (Ephesians 5:33)

This verse is also the third time in this section that Paul tells men to love their wife.

As a man with lots of male friends, I can say with a large degree of confidence, and not in a condescending way, that men don't have a clue about how to be men in our culture. And, most of us men are selfish. I'm not talking about being a macho man filled with ego. I'm talking about being a strong, humble, tender, mature, secure, loving man; like Christ. I'm a pretty confident guy, and still much aware of the time I am internally intimidated.

It is common, I think, for a man to admit, "I do not know how to give up my ego and the things I use to try and prove my identity in the world. I also do not know how to sacrifice and channel my efforts toward my wife so SHE gets attention. I am not secure and formed enough to do that!" It can be terrifying.

So, listen, when a man gets a vision for wanting to rise up and lay his life down for his wife, he's going to be awkward when he does it. From vision to execution, there is sometimes a disparity. It is hard to make noble attempts toward servanthood in the face of our pride, ego, comparison to others, and insecurity! (And every man just secretly said, "Amen!") So, wives, if you see your husband making an effort toward the right direction, give him some respect and encouragement. If he tries to serve you by cleaning up the house a bit, don't say, "Is that it?" Rather, say, "Your cleaning game is STRONG! Let's see what else you got!"

Husbands respond to wives who respect and encourage them, not insult or treat them in a condescending way. Spirit-filled mutual submission for wives, at least in part, looks like letting him love you. And when he tries, if you expect graduate level performance and get middle school results, be supportive and encouraging. Cultivate your respect for him because you'll be staggered by what you reap.

You ask, "How do I do that?" Just as with your husband, you can't on your own. But you can move in that direction because you have the life and power of the Holy Spirit in you.

> [32] This is a profound mystery — but I am talking about
> Christ and the church. (Ephesians 5:32)

When husbands and wives submit to and love each other well, it is a powerful pointer for others toward Christ and the Church.

Here's a great marriage question: How does your marriage keep telling the story of Jesus and the Church?

The point of marriage is ultimately to point to Jesus and the Church! How I long for someone to look at Cory and our marriage or your marriage and say, "What is THAT? Why do you love your wife like that?" And, for you or me to say, "We are swept up into something WAY bigger than us...the redemption of the entire universe. We and our marriage are a little preview of that redemption. The way I love my wife is pointing to the way Jesus loves me and loves the Church."

Or, husbands, how about someone asking Cory or your wife, "Why do you treat and talk about him like THAT?" And for her to say, "I am modeling something. There is a thing called the Church and it loves Jesus. How I respond to my husband is pointing to THAT." It's a preview of THAT.

This is some challenging stuff. It was controversial and subversive in the midst of the Greco-Roman world, and it is the same in ours today.

A couple of closing thoughts.

There are no cookie-cutter marriages. Mutual submission in this way is a huge canvas to paint on. Paul leaves out lots of details about everyday life. Every marriage has to go through the work of assessing strengths and weaknesses, getting creative, praying through it, fighting for unity on every front, and following Jesus.

<u>As a husband or a wife, we are to pay attention to the instructions to YOU</u>. I invite the Holy Spirit to speak to me about how I love Cory, and I have plenty to concern myself there for the rest of my life. I don't need to be telling her what to do. I am accountable before Christ for ME and MY part, not for hers. My duty as Cory's husband is to love her in a way that points to the way Christ loves the Church, not to remind her of her duties.

Next, I think it is healthy to regularly ask ourselves, "<u>Is my spouse thriving or flourishing? If so, is it in spite of me or because of me?</u>" For me, I hope Cory is saying, "Because I married Josh, this and this is what is happening in my life!" Or, is she saying,

> "Well, you know, God says in Romans Chapter 8 that all things work together for the good of those who love God; even this marriage. And, in James chapter 1 it says to consider it pure joy when you face trials and tribulations of many kinds because the testing of your faith in this marriage for 18 years has produced fruit."

Is Cory's thriving and flourishing enhanced because of me, or in spite of me? How can we take more and more steps to help each other reach our redemptive potential as we mutually submit to each other's love?

For those of you who are single, would you pray for married people once in a while?

I offer each husband and wife a 30 day experiment around today's passage and the following questions.

> 1) What would happen if we first submit ourselves to God, and then submit ourselves to each other in the ways described in this passage of Ephesians?

> 2) What new patterns and dynamics would we like to see occur in our marriage in the next 30 days?

You are free to disagree with all or part of what I have said. But, if you are married, you need to work at figuring out a theology and shared philosophy for your marriage. Life is too hard, and there is too much pressure and temptation to NOT go forward UNIFIED.

Practical note:

How do you make decisions in this type of marriage when you are not in agreement? I'm not saying this is the only way, but it is what Cory and I have come to. We press the pause button, pray, wait, and trust God to bring us to unity. This section of Ephesians is far more about unity than authority. It really presses into what we believe about God. If God has made the two of us one, He is big enough to bring us together. He can speak to me or my wife and unify us. I can honestly say that in over 18+ years of marriage, God has always brought us to unity. And those of you who know my wife know that it isn't because she just says, "Josh, whatever you want to do." Far from it! And sometimes achieving unity takes time! If, for some reason we just can't come together, our next step would be asking each other, "Who does this decision affect most?" That would influence our final decision.

Closing Prayer:

> God, I pray for your blessing on these marriages represented. Pour out your mercy. Unleash the power of your Holy Spirit over these marriages. We need your power as our living God to animate our marriages in our church with a Spirit-filled mutual submission. Build life, love, and intimacy into our marriages. Unleash your power in us to prefer one another, and change the culture and economy of our marriages. Unleash your power in us to walk humbly with one another in an attitude of submission and reverence for Christ. Let us reflect to our neighbors and the world the unity of Christ and the Church as we walk forward in the unity of love. We want strong growing marriages, and we pray that you will take us on another step of that lifelong journey today. In the name of Jesus we pray. Amen!

Subject: Re: Marriage Sermon on Ephesians 5:21-33 by Josh Miller; Pursuing Each Other

Rick and Georgeann, this is Jack.

Excellent sermon. Thanks for going to the trouble of getting it to us. What impressed me the most was how intentional God wants me to be in pursuing Caroline. And, how she is supposed to respond to me in the same way we are suppose to respond to Jesus who first pursued us.

A lot of my male friends seem to have this idea of pursuer and pursued backwards in their marriage. They act the same as when they were boys and their mother was the pursuer who cared for them. Somewhere between boyhood and manhood husbands are suppose to shift from the pursued, who are cared for by their mother, to the pursuers who care for their wife; and for that matter, the Church.

Caroline doesn't require much pursuit from me, but what she needs, she needs. And, meeting her needs fulfills my need to be the initiator and pursuer that God calls me to be. You have written before that since Caroline and I are both being conformed into our unique image of Jesus we should lay down our life for each other and love each other as we love ourselves. This means that when it comes to pursuing, sometimes I pursue her and sometimes she pursues me. Granted, I have a lot of catching up to do to come even close to matching her.

My last trip went well. We made it back this time without capsizing. When I fall off of a donkey I know what I am going to land in. When a canoe capsizes in this region you have no idea what is waiting for you. The last time it happened it terrified me, but our local team just laughed and took it in stride. I guess when a risk becomes a way of life for them, it no longer feels like a risk.

It always amazes me that when I arrive at a village the men and women are all smiles, and their children come running. Their kids are no different from Erica and Billy, other than the fact that they are malnourished and parasite ridden. I really don't understand how these believers keep growing in their faith because God's grace seems incredibly different here than back in the States. When I pray with them, they pray that I and my family would be blessed! I am ashamed to compare my prayers to theirs. I know you will say I should not compare myself to others, and I get it. But every time I come home, I can't believe I complain about anything. I so don't deserve to be in the same Body of Christ with these believers.

Caroline and I had some insight around my traveling. I noticed that things between us were often tense for a day or two before I would leave, and she would be standoffish for a couple of days after I got back. The first time I brought it up she thought I was just imagining things. We've since realized that the prospect of me leaving, triggers her abandonment issues from when Beth moved out to go to undergrad. That's when things at home got much more difficult.

Caroline also worries when I leave that I won't make it back. When I do, she is relieved that I am safe, but then withdraws because I have been gone. The dilemma is that she also believes in our ministry and wants me to go. She finally summed it up with, "I want you to go, but I don't want you to leave!" Isn't that strange? I think she needs to make up her mind whether or not we are in this ministry together.

We're going to go over Josh's sermon again. There's a lot of good stuff in it. Too much to take in on the first pass. When we get back to the States, hopefully we can visit Harvest and share what we are doing over here. It would be great to finally meet the two of you face to face.

Jack

Subject: Re: Re: Marriage Sermon on Ephesians 5:21-33 by Josh Miller; Pursuing Each Other

Jack and Caroline, this is Georgeann.

Pursuing

Jack, we equally pursue each other to the best of our ability, but we don't pursue each other equally. I put in more pursuit time by the clock than Rick because it's my nature. All of us need to become the best pursuers we can within the context of our background, strengths, weaknesses, and stage of growth. There will always be a mismatch. The important point, however, is you should not expect Caroline to do all of the heavy lifting. It would be silly for me and Rick to go to a health club and he expect me to lift his weights for him. We both need to lift what we can, and push ourselves in a healthy way to do more. When it comes to growth in any area, it's about what the Holy Spirit wants to do in you without condemning you for who and what you are not.

One of the ways Rick pursues me is by not *running away.* He can always find something "important" to do; especially when I'm in a bad mood. The pursuing I often need from him is to stay present with me. Look at me. Listen to me. Give me a hug. Ask if I need help. Be tender with our daughters. Tell me about his day or what he has been hearing from God. Be interested in what I have been hearing from God. He can even pursue me by telling me what he is struggling with as long as it isn't always and only about him.

Pursuit is so important because when Rick withdraws for extended periods, such as for a long-term project, I can feel abandoned and alone. I have grown to where I pick up on those feelings quickly and know it is time to check in with him and let him know what is happening. Early in our marriage, however, I would be confused, get angry, and either withdraw or lash out at him.

In some ways, our early struggles were not his fault because he didn't know any better. At the beginning of our third year of marriage I confronted him by saying, "We're going to have a good talk and you're going to have a good listen!" When he tells this story he says, "I sat there for forty-five minutes and finally said, 'You're right!,' because she was."

Jack, this is Rick.

Visibility

I get your concern about falling out of a canoe. What's the visibility over there? About a quarter inch? That's not a bad metaphor about life in general. Any visibility we think we have in life can just be a mirage.

One time I thought life was going pretty well until a large blood clot in my left calf muscle released and moved to my lungs. It evidently decided it was all grown up and wanted to become a bilateral pulmonary thrombus. I turned blue, passed out, and convulsed for a while. Just before that, I thought I had great visibility on my life. The only problem was that I ignored the warning signs of pain and swelling in my calf. We usually get these warning signs in all areas of our life, including marriage, and it is up to us whether or not to heed or ignore them. We ignore them at our peril.

Side note about blood clots: Don't forget to stretch your legs on long flights, or when sitting at a desk for long periods of time.

Deserving to be in the Body of Christ

As to the villagers, you wrote "I so don't deserve to be with them in the same Body of Christ." I agree with your sentiment completely, but also must point out that none of us deserves to be in the Body of Christ; except by God's grace and provision. In this regard, it is always good for me to invest time meditating on Ephesians 2.

> As for you, you were dead in your transgressions and sins, 2 in which you used to live when you followed the ways of this world and of the ruler of the kingdom of the air, the spirit who is now at work in those who are disobedient. 3 All of us also lived among them at one time, gratifying the cravings of our flesh and following

its desires and thoughts. Like the rest, we were by nature deserving of wrath. 4 But because of his great love for us, God, who is rich in mercy, 5 made us alive with Christ even when we were dead in transgressions—it is by grace you have been saved. 6 And God raised us up with Christ and seated us with him in the heavenly realms in Christ Jesus, 7 in order that in the coming ages he might show the incomparable riches of his grace, expressed in his kindness to us in Christ Jesus. 8 For it is by grace you have been saved, through faith—and this is not from yourselves, it is the gift of God— 9 not by works, so that no one can boast. 10 For we are God's handiwork, created in Christ Jesus to do good works, which God prepared in advance for us to do. (Ephesians 2:1-10)

In the light of this truth, Jesus says several times in the Gospels that the *first will be last, and the last first.* I'm fine waiting in line behind others in heaven, many of whom could be the villagers you described. I just want to make sure I'm in the right line!

Ambivalence

Caroline's statement, "I want you to go, but I don't want you to leave!"is profound. I know it may sound double-minded, but what she is experiencing is ambivalence. Before I received a Masters in Social Work, I thought ambivalence meant someone did not care about something either way. Actually, ambivalence means the opposite in that a person cares strongly both ways and is having difficulty deciding one way or the other.

Caroline strongly believes in your ministry together, strongly fears for your safety, and doesn't want to be left alone. And, from what Beth has told us about safety in your area, Caroline would be justified in her concerns. I guarantee you that if I were there telling Caroline that it would be best for you to travel into the jungle, she would counter with her concerns about your safety. And if I would tell her that you should play it safe and stay home, or even move back to the States, she would argue for continuing your ministry.

We all struggle with ambivalence, and the best way to help someone is to ask gentle, non-condemning, non-condoning questions. You don't condemn what they are thinking if you disagree, and you don't condone if you agree. You give them time to think and answer because they need to hear their own thoughts and answers, not be bombarded with what you think they should do. Your goal should be to bring their ambivalence out into the open so they can see it more clearly. You do this by asking questions about all sides of a decision. Be very careful when doing this that you do not get drawn into a debate or argument. One tool to use is a SWOT analysis where you ask about the Strengths, Weaknesses, Opportunities, and Threats of each option.

With Caroline, I would ask about her fears of you leaving for the villages (a Threat), and her satisfaction with the accomplishments of your ministry (a Strength and an Opportunity). I would ask about her relief of you staying home (a Strength of safety), and any regret she would have if you didn't go where she thought God was calling you (a Weakness by not following God's will).

Ambivalence and divorce

Beth and Bob really struggled with ambivalence regarding divorce. They both wanted one, and did not want one. We initially met individually and would ask questions such as,

"If you stay together, what challenges will you need to work through?"

> This could be viewed as a Strength in that Christians would stay together, an Opportunity to build their relationship, and a Threat of continued unfruitful pain if they didn't succeed.

"If you get divorced, what additional challenges will you face?"

> This could be viewed as a Strength in that the current pain stops, and a Threat that additional challenges will occur.

"If you get divorced, what pains go away, and what new pains begin?"

This could be viewed as a <u>S</u>trength in that the current
pain stops, and a <u>T</u>hreat that new pains could occur.

These SWOT labels are not nearly as important as the prayerful
thought that goes into the answers to these questions. In addition,
labels are not absolute and are relative to whomever is
considering them. Bob and Beth's children would have an entirely
different perspective regarding divorce as to what is a Strength,
Weakness, Opportunity, or Threat.

Bob and Beth both struggled with anger during our meetings and
when coming up with these answers. Bob's was often directed
inward resulting in him feeling depressed. Beth's was directed
outward, often towards us. When she would direct her anger
towards us, we just relaxed and sat tight. We have been doing this
long enough to know that anger directed *towards us* is not the
same as anger directed *at us*. Sometimes anger needs to be
discharged before thinking can begin.

We never answered Bob's repeated question of, "What would you
do?" We can't possibly know what we would do in any difficult
situation until we are in it. Our goal was to ask enough questions
that they could experience outwardly what they were struggling
with inwardly. What I admire about them is that once they
decided to work on themselves and their relationship, they were
committed to do whatever it took to build their marriage. They
never looked back. Even though they vacillated between the
stages of the power struggle and conscious marriage, they always
kept moving forward. When they felt the temptation to second-
guess themselves, they always made the same choice to stick with
it.

Before Bob and Beth began working on their marriage, they would
act like a couple in order to cover their wounds and shame. Now
they *are* a couple, and they support each other's healing and
growth. Neither would say their life and marriage are easy
because they still face challenges. Even so, they refuse to give up
any of the progress they have worked so diligently to achieve.

Anger

I keep getting a recurring thought so I will cover it in this email. Beth is labeled by the family as the one with the "anger" problem. In reality, Bob was just as angry as Beth, though he was much more composed about it. He can appear passive in his aggression.

Bob knew, and still knows, what sets Beth off. It's easy for everyone to see her anger, yet miss the ways Bob would provoke her. If anything, Beth should be commended for forcing their issues into the open. To her credit, and consistent with Josh's sermon, when Bob would take small steps of communicating his feelings in truth and in love, she would respond with acceptance and affirmation.

A big area of growth for Bob came when he saw us model how to be neutrally engaged with Beth when she was angry. When she acted threatening, we did not have to feel threatened. He learned he could stay present with an angry woman and would not die. As a result, when he knew she was upset, rather than cower and withdraw, he would stay present and face her emotions directly.

Walking towards the fire

I will paraphrase something Bob said that I will never forget because his imagery was so vivid. He said that dealing with her anger was like walking towards a fire.

> "If my left cheek felt cooler than my right, I would turn more to my right. When it burned equally on both sides, I knew I wasn't turning away. If I needed to continue walking into her anger, I could and would. If I needed to stand, I could and would. If she needed time and space, I could and would give it to her without feeling insecure."

I don't think this applies to you and Caroline, but tuck it away because it might be useful someday for a couple you are helping.

Have a blessed day,

Rick

Subject: Anger and Fire

Rick and Georgeann, this is Caroline.

What you wrote about Beth's anger and fire used to be true about Jack most of the time. He is better now, but we still struggle in this area. His intensity is intimidating for me and the kids, even if he doesn't say anything. When I bring it up he gets mad because he claims there is nothing he can do about it. Once he said, "If I'm not taking my anger out on you, you have no right to be upset by me being angry!" But by then, I was really upset because he was yelling at me.

When he gets angry, I feel completely intimidated and worthless. I can't even think straight. I know that isn't fair to him because he has grown in this area. Jack, you really have and I appreciate you so much for it!

My problem of intimidation in the presence of anger isn't only with Jack. During one of my women's Bible studies a husband of one of our members showed up and was really upset about something. They went outside and he was talking too fast in their native language for me to understand. I felt my body tighten up and my emotions started going crazy. I wanted to intervene, or help, or yell, or anything to make them stop. She didn't seem to need my help because she argued right back at him on everything he said. This went on outside for about five minutes and then they got quiet. Even though I kept teaching, I could hear them talk calmly for another minute or two. When she came back in she seemed like everything was fine. I was a wreck, but she was fine! Even thinking about it makes me uncomfortable. Am I weird?

Caroline

Subject: Fight, Flight, Freeze, Submit, or Stand

Caroline, this is Rick.

In your last email you asked, "Am I weird?" After careful consideration, we have concluded that the answer to that question is, "Yes."☺ But then again, we are all *weird* in our uniqueness and how conformed we are to the image of Jesus. My version of Psalm 139:14 is, "I praise you God because I am fearfully and weirdfully made; your works are wonderful, I know that full well."

Patterned reactions

People are who they are for reasons. Unfortunately, some people think reasons are excuses. They are not excuses; they are insight.

Part of the reason for your reaction to Jack's intensity and anger started long before you met him. In another email we wrote about how during childhood and young adulthood people build an Imago. Recall that it is a subconscious image of what you desire, and with which you are familiar. It is derived from relationships with people who were influential in your life. Beth is a significant contributor to your Imago that was activated when Jack came into your life. You likely were instantly comfortable with Jack because you had developed similar relationship patterns with Beth.

Both Beth and Jack are hard-charging specifists with extremely high standards. They both have a strong sense of purpose and commitment. They are both sensitive to criticism because of their own insecurities and self-doubt. They can both be very loving and very attacking. Lots of parallels between the two.

I would imagine that when Beth was angry, you would withdraw and become invisible. And, Beth's excellence in everything may have left you feeling inferior; even though you are amazing in Beth's eyes. She admires how balanced you are. She sees you as mentally and emotionally intelligent, giving and loving towards your children and others, and someone who lives out her faith. One time when we were talking about you she gave me a serious look and said in her typical Beth style, "Caroline impresses me." That's high praise coming from her.☺

In your last email you wrote, "My problem of intimidation in the presence of anger isn't only with Jack." You don't have a *problem*; you have a *pattern*. You more accurately could have written, "My *pattern* of intimidation in the presence of anger isn't only with Jack." A problem can be solved; patterns must be replaced.

Fight, flight, freeze, submit, or stand

Social science has known for years that people have a limited number of patterns for responding to a situation that feels threatening. The first two responses were called Fight or Flight. People either fought or would flee. Later, the concept of Freeze was added. People didn't fight or flee, rather, they froze and didn't do anything. Social science matured even further in this area and Submit was added. People often submitted to a threat and obeyed any demands. Ephesians Chapter 6: 10-20 adds another option which is to Stand.

> Finally, be strong in the Lord and in his mighty power. [11] Put on the full armor of God, so that you can take your stand against the devil's schemes. [12] For our struggle is not against flesh and blood, but against the rulers, against the authorities, against the powers of this dark world and against the spiritual forces of evil in the heavenly realms. [13] Therefore put on the full armor of God, so that when the day of evil comes, you may be able to stand your ground, and after you have done everything, to stand. [14] Stand firm then, with the belt of truth buckled around your waist, with the breastplate of righteousness in place, [15] and with your feet fitted with the readiness that comes from the gospel of peace. [16] In addition to all this, take up the shield of faith, with which you can extinguish all the flaming arrows of the evil one. [17] Take the helmet of salvation and the sword of the Spirit, which is the word of God.
>
> [18] And pray in the Spirit on all occasions with all kinds of prayers and requests. With this in mind, be alert and always keep on praying for all the Lord's people.

[19] Pray also for me, that whenever I speak, words may be given me so that I will fearlessly make known the mystery of the gospel, [20] for which I am an ambassador in chains. Pray that I may declare it fearlessly, as I should. (Ephesians 6:10-20)

When we stand in the power of the Holy Spirit, we do not have to fight, flee, freeze, or submit.

Choosing to stand or submit can seem confusing based on what Jesus said in Luke Chapter 6 about what to do with our enemies, and, according to John Chapter 2, what He did to the money changers in the temple.

Luke

"But to you who are listening I say: Love your enemies, do good to those who hate you, [28] bless those who curse you, pray for those who mistreat you. [29] If someone slaps you on one cheek, turn to them the other also. If someone takes your coat, do not withhold your shirt from them. [30] Give to everyone who asks you, and if anyone takes what belongs to you, do not demand it back. [31] Do to others as you would have them do to you. (Luke 6:27-31)

John

When it was almost time for the Jewish Passover, Jesus went up to Jerusalem. [14] In the temple courts he found people selling cattle, sheep and doves, and others sitting at tables exchanging money. [15] So he made a whip out of cords, and drove all from the temple courts, both sheep and cattle; he scattered the coins of the money changers and overturned their tables. [16] To those who sold doves he said, "Get these out of here! Stop turning my Father's house into a market!" [17] His disciples remembered that it is written: "Zeal for your house will consume me." (John 2:13-17)

In Luke, *standing* was manifested by intentionally blessing, praying, and giving even more than what was asked. In John, *standing* was manifested by attacking and driving them out. Both were done only in submission to the will of God in the power of the Holy Spirit.

This brings me to how you should respond to anger, Jack's in particular. You need to seek God to know when to *stand and give even more*, or *stand and defend* by setting a boundary. Either way, you are always to do your best to speak the truth in love.

Practical tips for responding to someone's anger

Here are three practical tips for interacting with someone who is angry. One is to give the appearance of eye contact by looking directly at the bridge of their nose. If you look directly into their eyes, your mirror neurons may start resonating with theirs, which can result in you getting more and more activated and losing control of your feelings. Staring at the bridge of their nose keeps you from having to look away when you feel intimidated, and prevents the age-old, "Look at me when I'm talking to you."

Another is to picture a full-length clear Plexiglas shield between the two of you, and watch their angry words hit it like projectile vomit. The distance between you and the shield makes you feel less connected and safer. Put a gutter at the bottom if needed. ☺

When you are on the phone, set it to speaker and place it two or three feet away. The physical distance gives you more perspective than when the person is injecting their venom directly into your ear. Also, don't use video with someone who is routinely angry. The point is that you need to maintain your perspective, and not get mentally and emotionally drawn into their anger.

Georgeann can stand in what she calls a "safe place" by putting on the full armor of God in the power of the Holy Spirit. She thinks, "No, you can't touch me with your anger." She stays engaged, just not on their terms. She also has a "look" that she saves for the very worst offenders.

Take care,

Rick

Subject: I Married My Sister!

Rick and Georgeann, this is Caroline.

So I am "weirdfully made" and I married Beth! That's a great way to start my day. ☺

Jack and Beth are incredibly alike and you don't know the half of it. Even though I idolized her, I can also remember how frustrating she could be. She always had her way of doing things. She used to argue with Dad constantly because he was always coming up with *his* way that he thought was better for some reason or another. Maybe "argue" is too strong of a term, but there was always a debate when those two were involved. I have no doubt that Dad and Beth loved each other because they are still really close.

I never wanted to confront either of them, so I usually gave in and did things their way. After a while I avoided conflict by learning to anticipate what either would want. It's the same way I used to be with Jack. Hmmm. This is a bit awkward. Sounds like I married Beth and my Dad! That's unfair though because Jack is not the way he used to be. He's really been growing a lot. For that matter, so have I. We've both been changing our patterns.

I've also been trying to be less defensive and critical. When I feel frustrated, I have been asking myself, "Why am I feeling this way?" It's pretty much the same as we did with the kids when they were growing up and would hit each other. We would say, "Use your words. What are you feeling?" Now after working through these emails we can also ask ourselves, How old do I feel emotionally? When have I felt this way before? What is the youngest age I remember feeling this way? Not sure we will ever grow up.

I've also used a different pattern for when we go on walks. Jack, if you haven't noticed what I have been doing, don't read this because it has been working.

I used to be so happy to be on a walk with Jack that I would chatter away continuously about my day and all matter of other things. Eventually I would ask him about his. He would just say, "Fine." By then he was completely tuned out because of my constant talking.

Now when we start our walk I stay pleasant and quiet for awhile just enjoying his company. Eventually I ask him about his day and he usually talks away. The key is that at the beginning of the walk I let him relax and collect his thoughts. Then when I ask a question, he's ready to respond. When he's finished, he always asks how I am doing. We both get to talk and listen. I don't know how helpful this technique would be to others, but it works for us. I discovered it totally by accident when Jack and I were on a walk and I was suffering from an extremely sore throat. All of a sudden I realized he had been jabbering away non-stop!

I was sharing with a friend of mine how Jack and I go on walks together, and she said that walking is good because men don't like sitting still and being face to face when talking. They prefer the less threatening side-by-side walk, or a drive in the car where they are allowed to keep moving and look around while listening. Who knows what all men want or don't want? I know we shouldn't generalize. One time Jack said that he wished I had come with an instruction manual. I replied that if wives did, most husbands wouldn't read it! Then again, he's the exception. He reads instruction manuals like they were the most recent bestselling novel.

I'll close for now. Need to prep for my next women's Bible study.

Blessings,

Caroline

Subject: Spinning Plates

Rick, this is Jack.

Nice tips on handling people who are angry. Georgeann's approach of standing firm is strong. As to the tricks, if we both know them, they aren't tricks! I can hear Caroline now. "Are you looking at me, or are you just staring at the bridge of my nose?!"

When we first started emailing back and forth, you asked me a question about spinning plates. I know you remember, and I appreciate you not pressing me on it. Yes, I did look at everyone like they were spinning plates that demanded I keep them spinning. Caroline, Erica, and Billy were three of those plates and God was another. I was even one of my own plates that I ignored until the last minute, and then lashed out at others when I was wobbling. I'm not proud of this, but I am doing better.

I ran from one person-plate to another for many reasons. For one thing, I needed to be needed. If I am needed, that means I am valuable to someone and they won't abandon me. I never knew it before, though I think I did deep inside, but I just couldn't put it into words.

When people need you, they are usually glad to see you. Unfortunately, it didn't always make me glad to see them. And, it wasn't that they were always glad it was *me*. It could be *anyone* as long as they got what they wanted. I no longer need to be needed. I am content with *wanting* to be needed because I want to serve God, my family, and others in a way that matters and makes a difference. I want to be about what God is doing.

I also see Caroline differently. She isn't a plate that I keep spinning to keep her functional. She is a plate from which I am fed. When I invest my life in her, I am also investing in myself and our children. I'm also investing in anyone she invests in. It is the same for her investing her life in mine. I'm not saying I still don't have people-plates that I have to keep spinning, it's just that I finally see that my wife and children are not those plates. And, I now realize that God is not one of those plates either.

I must confess that when we first started working with you and Georgeann, your emails were just more plates for me to deal with. When I look back at my replies, when I did reply, they were short and I was conveniently on the run. I thought Caroline and I were just in another rough spot that I had to ride out the same way I always did. Caroline is an amazing woman and I am grateful that she had the courage to see and deal with what God was showing us. It was exactly what I was ignoring.

Thank you for your patience.

Jack

Subject: Unfinished Business

Rick and Georgeann, this is Caroline.

After I read Jack's email I broke down in tears. His willingness to address the question of spinning plates and his desire to stop avoiding our problems made me realized that I have some unfinished business with you. It is Tim. I'm not going to go into everything, but I can share with you where I am at this point.

Tim was horrible to me growing up...and still is. When Beth left for undergrad he was a sophomore in high school and I was in seventh grade. Even though he always picked on me, it got much worse after she left for college. He constantly told me I was ugly and stupid. This came from a guy who was far from pleasing to look at and barely maintained a C average.

Tim has constantly been in trouble for as long as I can remember. Shortly after Beth left he did drugs more and more, and started shoplifting to pay for them. When he got caught, the family would be in turmoil for weeks. He often went through my backpack looking for money. No one could trust him.

What made me even angrier was that he would try to come into the bathroom without knocking and then act like it was an accident saying it didn't matter because we were family. Several times I caught him outside my bedroom window trying to look in. He would claim that he heard something outside and wanted to make sure I was safe. I told my parents a couple of times and they said they would talk to him. Even though they did, nothing ever changed. I finally stopped bringing it up. There's a lot more about Tim from when I was younger, but I'm too angry, not ready, and ashamed to go there. I just don't want to leave you completely in the dark.

Thank you for being understanding.

Caroline

Subject: Re: Unfinished Business

Caroline, this is Georgeann.

First, thank you for letting us know more about Tim. We learned a lot from Beth, but I'm sure she doesn't know some of the things you mentioned. At least she never told us about them. We think you and Beth need to talk about this when you are ready. She knows more details about Tim's childhood than your family has been willing to tell you.

Second, you have every right to be angry. What Tim did has no justification whatsoever. It is important for you to find someone you can regularly meet with to work through your anger at your own pace when you are ready.

Forgiveness is an exchange

Too often we have seen well-meaning friends recommend that people cover these kinds of experiences with a "blanket of forgiveness." That may work for a few, but it rarely deals with the ongoing consequences, and can be the same as denial and sweeping it under the rug. To effectively forgive someone, we believe that in most cases, you need to embrace the pain of the offense and identify exactly what you are forgiving. If you don't, unprocessed details may continue to come to the surface.

Danny Meyer, a Vineyard pastor, teaches in his Gospel of Wholeness series that forgiveness is an exchange with God. You place the offender, offense, and consequences in the hands of God, and He offers His peace and power back to you in return. It is a trade that leaves the offender in God's hands. You aren't *letting go* for the offender to run free. You are giving the offender, the offense, and the consequences to God so you don't have to carry them, or let them distract you from moving forward with your life. The offender's fate is in God's hands; not your thoughts.

This making a trade with God sounds straight forward, but is far from easy. Even if you trade something for God's peace, there are often habitual thought patterns such as bitterness, vengeance, and even self-loathing that can remain. Working to identify those patterns and bring about change takes time and often requires help from others such as a qualified counselor.

I have to be honest about this placing into God's hands thing. My fingers must be sticky because I regularly have to keep doing it with some of the same stuff. I know I have taken something back from God when I realize that my peace is gone.

Carrying someone else's shame

You wrote that you were too "ashamed to go there." From what I read, any shame you feel about Tim is not yours. You were a powerless child. The shame that is on you is Tim's shame that he has been unwilling to accept, and possibly anyone else's shame who knew and did not do what was necessary to protect you and help him.

When Billy and Erica come in from a day of playing outside, you don't look at the dirt that is on them and say, "You are dirt!" Or, "Look at that dirt that oozed out of you!" No. The dirt is *on them, not of them*. When they wash it off, they are free of it. Tim's dirt of shame is *on you*; it's *not you*. Whenever you feel that kind of shame, take it straight to God for a trade. For Tim's sake, I hope he responds to God and repents so he can get the help he needs. Even if he does, it is up to you to determine what kind of relationship you are willing to have with him, if any, in the future. As I mentioned, Beth knows some things that may be helpful.

I am writing in general now. You are not unusual in carrying someone else's shame. I've heard Rick explain it this way. When children are powerless and living in the midst of mentally, emotionally, spiritually, and/or physically dangerous people, they have one of two choices. The first is to believe that they are good, and are living in the midst of bad and dangerous people. The second is to believe they are bad, and are living in the midst of good and loving people. Most children choose the second option because it is less terrifying to think, "I am bad, and living in the midst of good people who love me."

It is also difficult for children to learn how to handle shame appropriately when others around them are condemning them and blaming them for things that are not their fault. As a result, these children carry the shame of the family system and grow into adults who think they are fundamentally bad.

It takes time as an adult to sort through painful memories, own what is yours, reject what is not, ask for forgiveness, and place the rest in God's hands.

I must warn you that family systems really don't like it when their shame bearer refuses to do his or her assigned job. Ultimately, it is about you taking a stand for who God created you to be, and against what others have put on you. This requires a renewing of your mind. I know that after all of these emails you remember Romans 12:1-2, but I will still include it.

> Therefore, I urge you, brothers and sisters, in view of God's mercy, to offer your bodies as a living sacrifice, holy and pleasing to God—this is your true and proper worship. 2 Do not conform to the pattern of this world, but be transformed by the renewing of your mind. Then you will be able to test and approve what God's will is—his good, pleasing and perfect will.

The "Do not conform to the pattern of this world" could just as well have been, "Do not *continue to be deformed* to the pattern of this world." Your healing and growth is completely obvious to us. You and Jack are on the right path and we encourage you to keep doing what you are doing.

In Him,

Georgeann

Caroline, This is Rick. I deeply appreciate your courage and trust.

Subject: An Odd Question

Jack and Caroline, this is Rick.

I've been talking with Georgeann and she says I should just come out and ask you this question. She finished her last email with, "You and Jack are on the right path and we encourage you to keep doing what you are doing." So here goes, what the heck are you doing?

When we started, you told us you were having a lot of arguments. Where are they? It isn't that I'm disappointed. I'm just wondering what happened? Are the two of you not having disagreements anymore? Or, are you just not telling us about them?

Just curious and hopefully pleasantly surprised,

Rick

Subject: Re: An Odd Question

Rick and Georgeann, this is Jack.

Sorry to leave you with the impression that we aren't having disagreements because we have plenty. Like Bob and Beth, we just don't let them build into arguments. When either or both of us gets tense, we have a checklist of the usual suspects that could be contributing to our angst. It isn't something we have formalized on paper. It just emerged as we worked through your emails.

The biggest cause of our disagreements is often the chaos of life itself. There is so much going on that we are always pulled in many different directions. We get tired, frazzled, frustrated, and then boom; a disagreement pops up. We ask ourselves, "Is it us, or is it life that is draining us?"

We also have to be careful that our observing ego has not been a harsh and critical judge with negative and accusing self-talk about the past or present. If so, we try to bring grace and truth into our thinking.

When one of us speaks or answers sharply, the other can either react or respond. It is our choice. How do we want the disagreement to end? How do we want our day or evening to go?

We also need to be careful not to slide back into the power struggle. This often happens when we feel vulnerable and lack power in other areas of our lives. If I feel out of control and disrespected at work, I must resist the temptation to come home and be excessively controlling in order to soothe my ego. When I am *demanding* of respect at home, it usually means I am not receiving what I think I deserve elsewhere, or even from myself. We try to keep our conflicts in their own arena. Work conflicts are dealt with at work and home conflicts are dealt with at home.

When we find ourselves in an argument, one of us must have the courage to call, "Timeout!" If the other does not heed our agreed upon strategy, then he or she is immediately declared the loser. In essence, the loser is saying, "No! I won't stop arguing! I'm going to keep yelling at you!" That's just childish.

A real change has also occurred with my pride. In the past, it wanted to win an argument at all costs and get Caroline to agree with whatever I wanted. Now, my pride is tied to me wanting to follow our rules of engagement.

Sometimes when we are having an argument, we will stop and eventually go through the formal process of letting one person talk with the other mirroring back what was said. It is tough for the listener to be limited to those two questions, "Did I repeat that back correctly? and "Is there more to that?" To be honest, we both struggle with the mechanical nature of this, so we'll do almost anything to not get to that point. I guess by that measure, it really does help us communicate better. It's there if we need it.

We have become much better at observing ourselves and each other. We have become comfortable with applying a well-placed hug at the right time. We also stopped being afraid of each other's anger and fears. Once they were understood, we became more fully available to each other. That was huge for me.

Many times Caroline's anger originates from frustrations during the day, or is the result of me taking her for granted. I have learned that when she does get mad at me for something, she will come back to me emotionally once we work things out. It's really just a question of how long we want to stay apart and if I am willing to be intentional about pursuing her.

A big revelation for us was that sometimes our differences were just a clash between our unique expressions of God's character, along with our different areas of healing and growth. We don't have to manipulate each other into our own likeness. We need each other's unique expression of God to be fully expressed and experienced.

A lot started changing when we decided to operate from the assumption of trust. We trusted that the other had our best interests at heart. And, we trusted that God could heal us when we were wounded by the other.

Understanding our core childhood wounds is also helpful. I know that Caroline's two core wounds are thinking she is not smart and feeling like she is invisible to others. It is my desire to encourage her and demonstrate how precious, intelligent, and visible she is to me. I can't make up for her past wounds, but I can do my best not to reinjure them, or create new ones. It is the same for her with me. She knows I am sensitive to acceptance and performance issues. She knows I can be a specifist. Even so, she loves me as I am, knowing I am striving to be better.

We've also learned that at times we need distance from each other so we can move closer. We both need our space and solitude. This means that I can watch Billy and Erica for an afternoon or a day while she invests time with the Lord and herself.

Another revelation is that we are not the enemy. That doesn't mean we won't hurt each other, but we have vowed to try and never let it be our intent. Even so, we still have to be intentional and careful in our interactions.

We also believe that God has given us stewardship of the other. He wants us to help each other become who He wants us to be. He wants us to be encouragers, not stumbling blocks. We are partners in each other's healing, growth, and ministry.

I'm sure there is more, but that's all I could come up with off the top of my head. I'll ask Caroline and see what she wants to add.

This is Caroline.

I agree with everything Jack wrote. For me, I have realized that I can give Jack space to figure out his tensions and grumpiness. When he is trying to work something out, he withdraws for a bit and needs time to think. I don't need to be pursuing him based on my insecurities, or make uninvited suggestions on what he should do. When he wants to talk about something, he will. It's the same with me. We resist the urge to tell each other what to do.

I am getting skillful at asking meaningful questions and waiting for his answers. The questions aren't meant for him to answer to my satisfaction, rather, his answers are to help him think it through. We have both become good at this and trust each other to do it well. Sometimes we fall into advice giving, but it usually takes no more than a wry smile by the other to communicate what we are doing. That said, we also give each other the green light by saying, "Ok, I'm done. What are your thoughts?"

I have also eased up the pressure on myself to be the perfect wife and mother, and to have the perfect home. I was serving an internal judge, the unhealthy part of my observing ego, that was condemning me day in and day out for what I was either doing or failing to do.

I think the greatest change in me was realizing that my desires and needs were important not only for me, but for Jack and our relationship as well. They could be God's whispers calling Jack into a place of growth and wholeness where he would not have thought to go on his own. Jack's desires and needs can serve the same purpose for me.

The big deal for us is that now we try to walk together in the same way that Adam and Eve walked before the Fall. He doesn't rule me and I don't seek to undermine him. We obviously still suffer from the consequences of the Fall, but we do not have to walk according to them.

We want God's will in our marriage as it is in heaven. My fullness in Christ does not threaten his or vice versa. I can admire him without feeling diminished. We don't see life as a zero sum game where he gets the recognition and praise and I don't. There's plenty of recognition and praise *for* both of us, and *from* both of us.

What is particularly freeing for me is that my identity is not wrapped up in his, or wrapped around his. I do not have to fight, flee, freeze, or submit out of fear or insecurity. I can stand wearing the full armor of God in the power of the Holy Spirit.

Jack and I also do not need to be ruled by patterns from our past. We can change them together. When Jack falls, I am there to minister to him as a fellow warrior. When I fall he does the same. When I am weak, he can be strong for us, and when he is weak, I can be strong for us. We live out Ecclesiastes 4:9-12.

Two are better than one,
   because they have a good return for their labor:
10 If either of them falls down,
   one can help the other up.
But pity anyone who falls
   and has no one to help them up.
11 Also, if two lie down together, they will keep warm.
   But how can one keep warm alone?
12 Though one may be overpowered,
   two can defend themselves.
A cord of three strands is not quickly broken.

And finally, we look at each day as another day to do marriage better. Our marriage is a unique expression of us and God in a way that has never been, nor will ever be again. We have committed to approach our marriage in the same way that the Apostle Paul did with his desire to know Christ.

Not that I have already obtained all this, or have already arrived at my goal, but I press on to take hold of that for which Christ Jesus took hold of me. 13 Brothers and sisters, I do not consider myself yet to have taken hold of it. But one thing I do: Forgetting what is behind and straining toward what is ahead, 14 I press on toward the goal to win the prize for which God has called me heavenward in Christ Jesus. (Philippians 3: 12-14)

Our marriage is part of our heavenward call.

Where we succeed, we praise God. Where we fail, we trust that our grace and mercy for each other, and His grace and mercy for us is sufficient. When someday all is said and done, and one of us has to say goodbye to the other, we want to know that we gave everything our flawed selves could give.

Hope this answers your question.

Love,

Caroline and Jack

Subject: Conflict Checklist

Jack and Caroline, this is Rick and Georgeann.

Your last email blew us away. We went through it step by step asking ourselves how we were doing in each area that the two of you mentioned. Some days great, others not so well.

Caroline, a while back when we were emailing about being a fixer or a facilitator, you wrote that you printed out a list of our suggested questions to help facilitate each other's thinking. You mentioned putting it on the refrigerator, or in a box on the wall with a glass front that said, "Break in case of emergency." Your last email is just as worthy of doing something similar.

What you and Jack wrote accounts for at least ninety percent or more of our arguments and those we have seen in others. You wrote that you have not formalized your checklist, so we have. We worked through your last email and others to create a list of questions for couples to consider when they are arguing...or more likely afterwards when they are trying to figure out what happened. It's not a matter of which one of these questions on the list will apply, rather, it's how many.

Conflict checklist

Is it us, or is it the daily pressures of life draining us?

Has our observing ego been condemning us?

Did one of us react rather than respond?

How do we want this disagreement to end?

How do we want our day or evening to go?

Have we fallen back into the power struggle?

Should we call a timeout?

Is our pride trying to "win" or "follow our agreed upon rules of engagement?"

Do we need to take turns talking and mirroring?

Are our fears or anxieties driving our behavior?

Are mental, medical, physical, or hormonal issues contributing to the conflict?

Does one or both of us need physical connection?

Is one of us really mad at or about something else?

Does this conflict involve our unique expressions of the image of Jesus?

Is this a recurring issue or pattern that needs healing and growth?

Have we lost trust in each other?

Is one or more of our core wounds involved?

Have we had enough personal time?

Do we see each other as the enemy?

Am I being a good steward of my spouse?

Does one or both of us need time and space to think?

Is one of us trying to be a fixer for the other?

Are we asking meaningful questions and waiting for answers?

Is either of us caught up in trying to be perfect?

Is this about a valid unmet need or desire?

Is one of us trying to rule over or control the other?

Is one of our strengths perceived as threatening by the other?

Are we taking a stand for what is right and godly?

Has one of us fallen and needs help?

Are we committed to making our marriage better as part of our heavenward call?

Everyone's marriage is under continuous and shifting pressures to which spouses either react or respond. Just as you wrote, when we think things are sailing along smoothly, something pops up. And if we are planning or worrying about the future, things get even more tense when we forget to take Jesus with us into those plans and worries.

We have struggles and arguments just like everyone else. To God's credit and glory, along with our efforts to be intentional in our interactions, they are far less frequent and not nearly as intense. Our faith in God, His wisdom, and the power of the Holy Spirit is what has delivered us to this point in our marriage and continues to sustain us. We also put into practice an adaptation of James 2:14-17.

Original

> What good is it, my brothers and sisters, if someone claims to have faith but has no deeds? Can such faith save them? [15] Suppose a brother or a sister is without clothes and daily food. [16] If one of you says to them, "Go in peace; keep warm and well fed," but does nothing about their physical needs, what good is it? [17] In the same way, faith by itself, if it is not accompanied by action, is dead. (James 2:14-17)

Our adaptation

> What good is it, my brothers and sisters, if Rick and Georgeann claim they want a great marriage but do not work at it? Can lack of effort produce one? [15] Suppose Rick or Georgeann has unmet desires or mental, emotional, spiritual, or physical needs. [16] If one says to the other, "Be happy; keep content, and act fulfilled," but does nothing about those unmet desires or mental, emotional, spiritual, or physical needs, what good is it? [17] In the same way, wanting a mutually satisfying marriage by itself, if it is not accompanied by action, is dead.

God does not give out mutually satisfying marriages, though He is always willing to help His children build them.

Let us know if you need anything.

Love,

Rick and Georgeann

ACKNOWLEDGEMENTS

We would like to thank Steve and Katie Helgeson who, during a presentation on marriage at Harvest Vineyard Church in Ames, Iowa, first exposed us to the idea that God's will on earth for marriage was best expressed when He created Adam and Eve, and not after He was forced by their actions to banish them from the Garden of Eden.

Thank you Ann Smiley-Oyen for working through a very early draft, and offering suggestions that considerably and justifiably increased our workload. Your sense of readability and structure is invaluable.

To our early draft and proof readers - We want to thank our youngest daughter Bonnie Mills and Lauren Horsch for their attention to story detail and grammar. We also want to thank Holly Greufe, Amy Gifford, and Kevan Flaming for their many suggestions.

A thank you is also in order for Jerod and Sarita Smeenk and their marriage home group where an early version of this novel was used for the first time in a group setting. Thank you Becca, our oldest daughter, for your guidance on structure and layout. We would also like to thank Mary L. Martin (Rick's mother) for her meticulous review of the final draft.

We are especially grateful to Stephen Judah of Columbus, Ohio who died June 21, 2008 of esophageal cancer at the age of 59. His marriage weekend seminar that we attended over thirty years ago provided the foundation that the Holy Spirit has used to transform our marriage. We learned of the seminar from our dear friends, Terry and Sue Castor, who cared for us and our three year-old daughter, Becca, during that very intense weekend. Their unwavering support for us personally and for our ministry is deeply appreciated.

We are also grateful to Josh Miller, Senior Pastor at Harvest Vineyard Church in Ames, Iowa, for his vision and support of our ministry. He has the knowledge and wisdom of a skilled teacher and the heart of a loving shepherd.

And finally, to the many couples over the years who have shared the sacred ground of their marriage with us, we are incredibly thankful for your courage, trust, and authenticity before God. Our marriage and life together is far better because of what we have learned from you.

May we all stay faithful on our journey to a mutually satisfying marriage.

In Him,

Rick and Georgeann

www.ingramcontent.com/pod-product-compliance
Lightning Source LLC
Chambersburg PA
CBHW071311250626
47159CB00004B/1383